Beneath the Willow

Jeremy Asher

D1403018

Editing and eBook formatting services provided by

Holloway House (hollowayhouse.me).

Prologue

Jesse

Jesse looked out the window of his New York apartment and watched as a man and a woman, standing on the sidewalk, moved into a kiss. Pedestrians flowed around them like water from a creek making its way around a rock, as if unaware of the miracle of love in front of them. Up until a week ago, Jesse would have considered himself one of those oblivious pedestrians, traveling through life with an agenda that included just about anything, as long as it had nothing to do with love. But things were different now. He was different. And for the first time, he realized that life had given him a second chance. One that he was determined to make the most of.

He grabbed the bouquet of roses he'd purchased from a street vendor on his way home and looked for a vase. After glancing through all of the cupboards, he gave up his search and settled on an old Coke bottle that had been used as a decorative piece. Then he lit the centerpiece candle on the table.

Today marked the last day of classes for his graduate program in architecture, and it was as good a reason as any to celebrate. Three years of studying through the night and cramming for exams had all boiled down to today.

When he walked out of his last class, Jesse had felt the sunlight on his face, kissing his skin with the warmth of its rays, and all he could think about was how much he wanted to share this moment with Kate Ashcroft, the one friend who had been there for him through the good and the bad.

Two years ago, Kate had left their hometown of Chicago to come to tap into the Big Apple's beauty market and open her latest salon. She had tracked down Jesse when she got to the city and they started hanging out together. Before long, they had agreed they could help each other out financially by sharing an apartment.

Sure, he had had his reservations at first. After all, they'd had a brief "friends with benefits" relationship before he left Chicago, and it could only be described as fire and ice, but that was old news. Moving in with Kate had meant no more sharing his old apartment with cockroaches, not to mention shaving about fifty minutes off of his daily commute to school and back. Besides, they had established the "rule." *Nothing more than friends.* And that had worked. School was his priority, and he couldn't let something as complicated as love or a relationship get in the way. He'd come too far and worked too hard to lose sight of his dreams. It had nearly happened to him once before, and he wasn't about to make that same mistake twice.

But, again, his life was different now. The weight of earning his master's degree finally lifted from his shoulders, he felt a sense of accomplishment. He discovered a clarity he hadn't experienced in three years and could envision his future. He could see clearly now what he'd been trying not to see these last few years: Kate. The way she smiled with her eyes. How she touched his arm whenever she laughed at something he'd said. She was all he could think about. She was all he craved.

The clock on the stove displayed the time: 5:50 p.m. Kate would be home any minute, so he tossed the pizza he'd picked up on his way home into the oven, warming it at a low temperature. Then he pulled out the bottle of red wine he'd been saving for a few weeks. Although Jesse rarely drank alcohol, he always kept a bottle of wine around just in case.

Flowers, candle, wine, and a pizza, everything seemed ready. He took a seat at the table, fantasizing about the look on her face as she walked through the front door to find the romantic scene he had set. He could hardly wait.

For two years, Kate had divided her time between Chicago and New York. Managing salons in both cities required a lot of juggling. All of her salons had been very profitable, but she favored the ones in Chicago. She said it was because of all the money they brought in, but he had suspected that it had more to do with being able to visit her family and friends when she was back home.

Jesse had only gone back to Chicago a handful of times since moving to New York for school. Too many memories. And too many disappointments. Sure, his brother and niece were in Chicago, but so were all those memories, and he'd just as soon leave them there. But now he had a decision to make: the Big Apple or the Windy City. As of today, New York was winning. But would Kate want that, too?

He checked his cell phone and the time at least a dozen times. An hour had passed with no sign of Kate. He walked over to the candle and drew in a breath, readying himself to blow it out, when the door opened and Kate walked in. He turned in anticipation, but stopped short.

A faint smile seemed plastered on her face. She walked over to the table. Calm, without so much as a glance at Jesse or the romantic scene he had prepared for her. It wasn't like her to be this quiet, or this…composed.

"Everything okay?" he asked.

She pulled out a chair and sank down, still seemingly unaware of the flowers or the candle. She nodded, and with a voice barely above a whisper, she said, "Yeah."

"What's going on? You're acting strange."

And that's when it hit him. A feeling he hadn't experienced in the past three years, weighing him down like a bag of bricks crushing his chest, causing him to sit down at the table. Was it happening to him all over again?

She held up her hand, revealing the large diamond perched on her finger. "I'm getting married."

Chapter One

Jesse

Chicago, three years later

Jesse let out a yawn as he rubbed his eyes. They burned from exhaustion, too many hours staring at a computer screen.

"You should take a break, boss." Jesse turned to see his assistant, Nina Lamont, walk into his office. She handed him a Starbucks latte.

Nina was an intern from the University of Chicago. His tiny company of one had begun to take off after its first year, and Jesse needed help with the day-to-day tasks around the office. He just couldn't afford much. Nina had arrived for the interview about twenty minutes early, wearing a suit and carrying a briefcase. Passion resonated in her voice when he had asked her why she wanted the job, reminding him of himself when he was just an undergraduate. She had been hired for the spring semester, but Jesse decided to keep her on for the summer as well. Her creativity and attention to detail reminded him daily how lucky he was to have her working for him.

"Thank you," he said, bringing the warm cup to his lips. "You're a lifesaver."

"I was serious about you taking a break. You've been working non-stop since you came in this morning. You should take a breather and get some fresh air," she said, taking a seat in the leather chair across from his mahogany desk.

"This bid is too important," he said, looking back at his screen.

She leaned forward and picked up a sketch off of his desk. "Renovating The Drake Hotel is an architect's dream," she agreed.

"Especially for a company as young as this. I know it's a long shot." He set his latte on the desk and stared at a photograph of the Chicago landmark. "But we might get lucky."

"No one knows Chicago as well as you. Your ideas are so…" She paused, studying the sketch in her hand. "You just have a way of capturing the true essence of this city. They would be foolish not to pick you." She placed the sketch back on his desk.

"Thank you. But you do realize that flattery isn't going to get you a day off, don't you?" Jesse said, smiling.

"Trust me, I do know that. And I wouldn't take one if you offered it." She pulled out her iPhone and slid her thumb across the screen. "I'm going to swing by the Lincoln Park project on my way home. I want to make sure that the guys are still on schedule."

"You don't have to do that. I can check it out later." He rubbed his eyes again.

"Really? And how are you going to meet Kate at the florist if you're busy checking out a site?"

"Oh no!" he groaned. "I completely forgot. What time is it?" He pulled back the cuff on his white shirt to look at his watch.

"Relax. It's only ten after five. You have about twenty minutes to get there. But I'd suggest that you get moving," Nina said, standing up. "Tell Kate I said hi."

"Sure." He sprang up from his chair and threw on a gray blazer before saving the document on his computer. Then he headed out the door. "Like I said, you're a lifesaver," he shouted.

"Remember that when it comes time to write me a recommendation letter!"

Jesse hopped in the back of a cab and gave the driver instructions to the floral shop on North Michigan Avenue. He pulled out the directions he had scribbled on a piece of paper when Kate had called him during lunch. On a day when he wasn't so rushed, he would have preferred to walk the mile and a half to the floral shop, but he knew Kate would already be there waiting for him.

The cab pulled in front of the shop and Jesse pulled out his wallet and paid the driver. The sign above read FLOWERS OF CHICAGO in a fancy cursive font. *This has to be it.* The floral shop occupied space on the bottom floor of a historic-looking building, reminding him of Sam's Pet Shop, the pet store his aunt and uncle had opened after his uncle had retired.

Jesse smiled thinking back to the days he spent in that pet store. He had worked there when he was an undergraduate still trying to figure out which path his life would take. It's where he had first met Kate. Her father owned the building, and she'd come with him one day when he had business to discuss with Jesse's uncle. Funny how that encounter eventually led him here, the place where they were about to put the finishing touches on their wedding plans.

Jesse opened the glass door and a potpourri of floral fragrances reminding him of the perfume section at Macy's hit him like a crashing wave when he walked inside. Flowers were arranged on clear shelves that lined the walls, leading to a mosaic of photographs showing off elaborate floral projects. A three-tiered display sat in the center of the store and overflowed with floral arrangements, teddy bears, vases, and balloons.

Jesse spotted someone familiar studying the medley of photographs splayed on the wall. Jesse walked up to her and placed his hands around her waist and then gently kissed the back of her neck. "You better be careful. My fiancé is going to be here any minute now," she said, slowly turning to face Jesse.

"In that case, I have this little place on West Elm Street where we can spend some time getting to know each other better," he said, giving her his best smoldering look.

"Hmmm," she said, playfully biting the tip of her finger. "How little?"

"Let's just say that it's big enough."

"Well, West Elm Street isn't exactly the North Shore, but does it at least have a view?"

"It has a view all right. We could make love on the roof terrace. It offers some of the best views of Chicago, as well as the lake. And if that doesn't work for you, then we can always make our own views." He pulled her close to him.

"Now you're talking." She leaned in and kissed him slowly on the lips. A kiss that reminded him of why he was marrying her. She smiled, and then smacked him on the shoulder. "What took you so long?"

"What?" he said, rubbing his arm. "I'm not late."

"You're not early either. I'm beginning to wonder if you're really into this wedding."

"Of course I am," he said, pulling her toward him again. "I've been busy."

"There you go again. Trying to seduce me with those gorgeous big blue eyes of yours."

He feigned surprise. "I'd never do that." Then he gave her a quick kiss on the lips. "Besides, my lips are where all of the seduction takes place."

"So, what do you think of this place?" Her arms spread open, as if displaying the entire store.

He scanned the shop one more time and noted the elegant flowers and the beautiful arrangements. Although Jesse's knowledge of flowers stopped at being able to tell the difference between roses and carnations, he had to admit that he hadn't seen flowers quite this beautiful before. "I think it's the perfect place to buy wedding flowers."

"You're just saying that to get this over with," she said, shooting him a suspicious look.

"Me? Never." He shifted weight to his other foot. "Seriously, I like this place. It's very charming."

"These right here," she said, pointing to a few photographs hanging on the wall. "These are some arrangements that they've done for previous weddings."

Jesse pointed to the top right photograph. The white flowers made the red roses pop, and the dark green leaves and baby's breath softened the look, making it simple, yet beautiful. "I like that one."

"That's one of my favorites," said a woman's voice from behind them. Kate turned around, but Jesse lingered a moment longer on the picture.

"Are you the owner?" Kate asked.

"Yes."

Jesse turned to face the woman and introduce himself, but words, as well as his breath, had left him.

That smile, those crystal blue eyes, the curly, long blonde hair. Jesse blinked to see if he was imagining it, but there she stood, smiling at him just as she had done when they were kids, and then again when she had walked into his aunt and uncle's pet shop six years ago. Sarah Ramsey stood in front of them.

"Jesse Malone?" the woman asked, taking a step closer and looking just as surprised as Jesse felt.

"Hello, Sarah." He held out his hand.

"It's been a long time, Jesse."

"A very long time," he agreed.

Kate cleared her throat. "So, you two know each other?"

"Uh, yeah," he said, breaking the handshake. "From a long time ago."

"You don't say. How long ago?"

Jesse turned to Kate. "We were…" He paused and glanced back at Sarah, still in shock at running into her after all this time. "Twelve," he said at the same time Sarah said, "Twenty-two."

"Well, twelve when we first met," Jesse explained. "Then twenty-two when we met again."

"Twenty-two?" Kate asked. "That was about six years ago."

12

Sarah nodded. "We grew up in the same small town, New Haven, Indiana, but he moved away when we were still kids. I didn't see him again until that day six years ago when I wandered into his uncle's pet store in Old Town."

"Really?" Kate said, looking at Jesse. "I don't recall you mentioning running into a childhood friend at the pet shop."

"Well, it was a long time ago," he said, forcing a smile. Jesse felt the tension filling the room like smoke filling a kitchen after a burnt meal.

"So, do you two like that one?" Sarah asked, changing the subject and pointing at the same photograph they had been commenting on.

"Yes," Kate said. "It's very simple, yet beautiful."

Jesse took a step back and watched as Kate and Sarah talked shop. He couldn't hear a word they were saying, not that he'd understand much of what they were talking about if he could. The moment felt surreal, like a dream. There had to be hundreds of flower shops in Chicago, and Kate had selected the one owned by Sarah, the only other girl he had ever loved. And the one girl who had shattered his heart when she decided to marry another man. But something didn't make sense. She had been planning on building a greenhouse and opening a plant nursery. *How did she end up with this place?*

He couldn't help staring as she spoke, as if expecting to wake at any minute. Her hands painted a picture as she described wedding flower options, creating a visual for Kate. Her long hair cascaded down her back like an exotic waterfall. Her black and red form-fitting dress ended just below her knees, revealing her tanned legs and four-inch heels. Her beauty was just as stunning as it was haunting. An image that had been impossible to forget, no matter how many years had passed or how hard he'd tried, was standing before him, like it was yesterday.

Kate looked at Jesse and pulled him back to her. "So, what do you think, Jess?"

"I say we go for it," he responded, not having a clue as to what he had agreed to.

"Do you think you will be able to have this ready for us by the end of September?"

"That doesn't give us much time," Sarah replied.

"I know, and I apologize for the short notice. You see, the florist we had scheduled had to back out due to a family emergency. And well, all of my friends have raved about the work you guys have done for people they know. I was so hoping that you'd be able to find time to fit us in."

Sarah opened a small red planner and flipped through the pages. "Let's see. Today's...August 23rd. I have a few rather large events at the beginning of September, but this will be simple enough. I should be able to fit it in."

"Let's do it." Kate wrapped her arms around Jesse. "It's going to be perfect," she said, smiling up at him.

"It was a pleasure meeting you," Sarah said, shaking Kate's hand. "I'll be in touch to get all the details about the date and location of the venue, and to confirm your selections."

"Sounds good," Kate said.

"It was good seeing you again, Jesse."

"Same here."

They headed for the door when Jesse glanced back, as if by instinct, and took one last look at Sarah.

He noticed something about her that nearly stopped his heart.

She wasn't wearing a wedding ring.

Chapter Two

Jesse

Kate did most of the talking during the cab ride home. Jesse listened and nodded when appropriate, but his mind kept drifting back to the flower shop. Back to Sarah. Although she looked just as beautiful as the last time he had seen her, she seemed…different. More professional. And more grown up, as if the last six years had been full of wisdom-building experiences. She definitely looked happy. But what had happened to the plant nursery? And where was her mother's ring? The one her father had left for her in the time capsule they'd buried together beneath the willow tree when she was a little girl. He remembered the day he and Sarah went back to New Haven to find it, after her father died.

"Are you listening to me?" Kate's voice brought Jesse out of his thoughts and back to the cab.

He nodded. "Of course."

Kate went on telling him about her day, which had consisted mostly of hanging out at one of the beauty salons she managed. She owned several in Chicago and held on to the few she had opened in New York when she and Jesse had lived there while he worked on his master's. Those locations required some traveling, but no more than a few weeks out of the year.

She brought up the lunch she had had with her father, Christian Ashcroft. He was a wealthy financial advisor who worked in the finance district. Over the years, he had earned quite a reputation, as well as a comfortable salary. For the most part, Jesse got along with him, although he sensed that Mr. Ashcroft wasn't completely sold on him.

Jesse's firm—if you can call a one-man shop a "firm"— was doing well, and he was making good money now, but he didn't come from a well-known, wealthy family, and he had a feeling that it was a point of contention with her father and probably always would be. But Kate was an outgoing and beautiful woman who had her father wrapped around her finger, right next to the two-carat ring that Jesse had given her when he proposed.

Jesse had figured, after living as friends and roommates for two years and then successfully dating for nearly three more, it was now time. Besides, his only stipulation before getting engaged was that he wanted to be able to stand on his own two feet and take care of himself as well as the woman he loved. And his little architectural design company had been doing well, better than he had anticipated.

"Jesse?"

"Huh?"

"You really are in La La Land today, aren't you?"

"Sorry, I'm listening. I've just got a lot on my mind with the Drake bid coming up."

She grabbed his hand. "You are totally going to get it. So, stop worrying about it."

"What makes you so sure?"

"Because you're brilliant, hardworking, and the most handsome man I've ever laid eyes on."

"You're biased." Jesse lowered the window a crack to let in some fresh air.

"So, tell me about Sarah."

"Huh? Sarah? There's not much to tell. We met in New Haven when I was twelve, but my family moved here shortly thereafter. So, we didn't really get to be friends. Then we ran into each other six years ago when she walked into Aunt Sherry's pet shop. And that's about it."

"Did you guys date?"

"Date? No, of course not. In fact, she had just gotten engaged as I recall. We got together a few times and caught up with each other, but then I moved to New York. I can't say I've really thought about her since. I assume she got married."

"Really?" Kate looked out the window. "That's strange. I didn't see a wedding ring on her finger." Jesse just shrugged as he tried to remain disinterested in the topic. "Anyway," Kate continued, "I thought she was pretty. I also think she likes you." Jesse noted a slightly jealous ring in her voice, one he hadn't heard before. Being both beautiful and successful made her a confident woman, never the jealous type.

"That's crazy," Jesse said, wanting more than ever to change the subject. "I'm sure your imagination is getting the better of you."

"Women have a sense about these things, you know."

"Is someone feeling a little jealous?" Jesse asked teasingly.

"Me? Now look at who sounds crazy," she said, crossing her arms.

Jesse slid closer and placed his arms around her waist. He leaned in and whispered, "I think someone's a little jealous. I think I'm going to have to do something about that when we get to the apartment."

"Yeah, like preparing me some of that delicious spaghetti you make."

"Anything you want." He gave her a gentle kiss on the lips.

"You're the sweetest," she said.

They were just a few blocks from their apartment when Kate's phone rang. He could tell by the conversation that it was her mother, and he knew that he could pretty much forget about starting dinner for at least an hour. Her mother, Laura Ashcroft, seemed to live for every detail of Kate's day.

Kate ran a hand through her dark, luminescent hair. It shone, reflecting the light, just like the hair of the celebrity models in those shampoo commercials. Beautiful was the only word that accurately described Kate. Like her mother, she had a thin frame that moved with grace when she walked into a room, turning heads everywhere she went. She never had to worry about dieting or carb counting. But she still enjoyed working out, claiming it gave her more energy. And although Jesse loved her hair, the tiny dimples that formed when she smiled, a trait she had inherited from her mother, were his favorite feature of hers. That smile drew people to her like hummingbirds to red sugar water.

Kate also had a flair for materials and status. A product of her upbringing. A trait she had inherited from her father, one that Jesse had a difficult time relating to.

When the cab came to a stop, Jesse paid the driver while Kate continued chatting on the phone with her mother. They walked through the lobby and rode the elevator to their apartment on the twelfth floor. Kate went into the bedroom. Jesse wandered into his office and took a seat at his desk.

He looked out his window and saw a man and a woman sitting beneath a tree, probably using the shade to avoid the August heat. The woman's long, curly hair reminded him of Sarah's golden waves. Of all the millions of people he could have run into in Chicago, he thought.

Seeing Sarah again after six years brought back a wave of memories. Jesse remembered the last night they had spent together—beneath the willow tree next to Crooked Creek. Waking next to her had been one of the best mornings of his life. He had no idea that the following day would be one of his worst. The day he would have to let her go, forever.

Seeing her now brought so many questions to mind: What happened to the greenhouse, Sarah? What happened to Kevin, the man you were going to marry?

Jesse heard a tap on his door, and he turned around to find Kate standing in the doorway. Her pink robe accented her curvy hips and thin waist. "I was thinking about taking a shower and freshening up before dinner. You want to join me?"

"I'd love to, but there's something I need to run out and do."

She untied the robe and let it open just enough to reveal the curve of her breasts. "Are you sure?"

Beautiful…definitely the only way to describe her. And her subtle seductive techniques were very effective. But there was something he had to do. And he knew that he wouldn't be able to concentrate on anything else until he settled this. "You are so incredible. But there's something that I just have to do first."

She walked into his office and sat on his lap. "You okay?"

He forced his best smile. "Yeah. I've just got a lot on my mind right now."

"The Drake?"

He nodded.

"Then do what you have to do." She ran a finger across his chin. "And when you get finished, I'll be waiting for you."

Chapter Three

Robbie

The tiny brass bell rang, announcing the arrival of another customer. It had been an unusually busy Monday for this time of year. Not that Robbie was complaining. He'd recently opened a second store, this one in the Lincoln Park area, so he definitely appreciated the business. Robbie set his clipboard on a shelf and headed for the shop entrance.

"You want me to get that, boss?"

"I got this one, Ricky. Can you keep an eye on the register?"

"Got it."

Ricky Everlee had been Robbie's best hire and saving grace. He showed up every day and stayed late when necessary, and he never complained about the work. He had been as dependable as the sun rising and setting each day.

When Robbie rounded the corner, he found Jesse staring at the cage of puppies. A warm and joyful sensation overcame Robbie. "Ponyboy?"

A smile formed on Jesse's face. A smile that looked just like their mother's. "I was just in the neighborhood and thought I'd stop by and say hello. See how things were going."

Robbie studied his face. The last time Jesse had visited his pet shop had been a few months ago. "Everything okay?"

"Yes. Can't a guy visit his brother and—"

"Uncle Jesse!" Madison shouted, nearly knocking Robbie over on her way to Jesse.

"Hey, Peanut." She leaped into his arms, like a frog shooting for a lily pad. Jesse caught her and held her suspended in the air as she smiled down at him. "You just get prettier and prettier every time I see you."

Her charcoal hair swung freely down the sides of her face. "What did you bring me?"

Jesse set her back down and reached into his jacket pocket. "What do you think I brought you?"

"Candy?"

Jesse brought out a chocolate candy bar. "Wow, you're a smart cookie." Jesse looked over at Robbie. "Just like your Uncle Jesse."

Fifteen years ago, Robbie would have put him in a headlock and waited for Jesse to say, "Robbie is the strongest, most good looking, and most intelligent person I know." But Jesse wasn't thirteen anymore. And he had filled out quite a bit over the years. Robbie wasn't too sure he could get him in a headlock anymore.

"May I please have it?" Madison asked.

"Well, that's up to your dad."

She turned to Robbie. Her bright green eyes pleaded with him.

Robbie just nodded.

"Thank you!" she shouted. She took the candy bar from Jesse and then gave him a huge hug.

"You're welcome, Peanut. I've missed you."

She ran over to Robbie and held up the candy bar. "Can I have it now?"

Robbie shook his head. "No can do, honey."

Her eyes narrowed and her lips curved into a frown.

"You have to have dinner first, baby. Why don't you go upstairs and get your pajamas on while I talk to Jesse a little while."

Her little arms wrapped around his legs and his heart. A hug he had grown to depend on ever since Felicia had passed away. Then she ran up the stairs to their apartment above the pet shop.

"She's getting so big."

"Yes, she is. You should stop by more often. She talks about you all the time."

Jesse looked down and rubbed his forehead. "I know. It's just hard with work and—"

"And the memories of this place?"

"I didn't say that."

"You didn't have to, Ponyboy. You've always been the sentimental one of the two of us. The sensitive one."

"Speaking of sentiment. There's something I wanted to talk to you about."

Robbie started for the back of the store, passing barking puppies along the way. A bench used for grooming dogs and cats sat at the back along with two stools where they each took a seat. "What's on your mind, little brother?"

Jesse looked down and kneaded his temples with his thumb and index finger. "It's been a long and crazy day."

"I can see that." Robbie knew about the Drake project and knew Jesse had some pretty good competition going in on the bid. But Jesse had talent, and architecture was one thing he had been passionate about ever since they were kids. "How's Kate doing?" Robbie figured Kate was as good a place as any to start, and whatever was bothering Jesse probably had something to do with women.

"She's great. Busy. With her beauty salons and the projects I have going on, we usually only see each other in the evening."

"Sounds really stressful."

"No. I mean, it would be nice to relax more, but we both love our jobs. Anyway, that's not what I came here for."

"Well, what's going on? Spit it out." Robbie watched the look on Jesse's face turn serious.

"I ran into Sarah today."

"What? Sarah Ramsey?"

Jesse nodded.

"Whispering Meadows Sarah? Where did you run into her?"

"At the flower shop where Kate and I were picking out flowers for the wedding."

"Talk about awkward."

"No kidding. We were just standing there looking at these photographs of flowers, and you know me, I don't know the difference from one flower to the next. I was just hoping it wouldn't take all night, and then Sarah walks up behind us and introduces herself."

"What? She works there?"

Jesse shook his head. "Worse. She owns the place."

"Wow. What a mind blow. I need a minute to process this information."

"You're telling me. You don't know how hard it was to pretend like everything was normal."

"So, Kate doesn't know?"

"She knows that Sarah and I knew each other in the past, but she doesn't know how well we *knew* each other. Was that a mistake?"

"What? Are you crazy? Of course it's not a mistake." Robbie rubbed his chin. "Besides, what good would that have done, telling her about how Sarah was the first love of your life and how you left Chicago all those years ago without ever saying goodbye to her."

"It wasn't like that."

"You know what I mean. All I'm trying to say is that it wouldn't have made things better. It's not like seeing Sarah again changes things between you and Kate."

Jesse didn't say anything. He didn't have to. Robbie read it in his eyes. The real reason why Jesse had stopped by his pet shop for the first time in months. It wasn't because he had seen Sarah after all these years. Or because he needed help picking out flower arrangements with Kate. It was because there was something weighing heavily on his mind. Something dark. "Kate's a good girl, Jess. Don't mess that up."

"I know that. I was just thinking—"

"I know you were thinking. I can see it in your eyes, and that *thinking* is going to get you into trouble. Kate loves you. And as for Sarah, well, she's the past, and that's where she should stay."

"Forget about it." Jesse stood up. "I should be going."

Robbie knew Jesse was hiding something from him. "What are you not telling me, Jesse?"

"Don't worry about it. It's nothing." Jesse put his hands in his pockets. "It's not why I came here."

"Then why did you come here?"

"Because I don't know if I should get married."

"You see." Robbie motioned to Jesse. "This is what you do, man."

Jesse's eyes narrowed. "What are you talking about?"

"You have no follow through when it comes to women."

Jesse turned. "I don't have to listen to this crap. Thanks for your help, big brother."

Robbie grabbed his arm and turned him around. "Stop running! Kate loves you very much. I see it every time she looks at you."

Jesse didn't say anything.

"Listen, I'm going to tell you something you probably don't want to hear." Robbie paused and took a deep breath. "You never follow through when it comes to relationships. You didn't follow through with Kate six years ago when you two first started dating. Then you didn't follow through with Sarah when you stood her up that day at the coffee shop."

"It wasn't like that," Jesse interrupted.

"Then what was it like?"

Jesse's shoulders dropped. "Just forget about it."

Robbie placed his hand on Jesse's shoulder. "You're my little brother and I love you, man. But you need to stop running. Kate's beautiful and fun and she loves you." Robbie took a step back and scanned Jesse. "I'm not sure what she sees in you. But hey, that's her problem now."

Jesse ran a hand down his tie. "She's got good taste."

"Sure, Ponyboy. You keep telling yourself that."

"I thought I told you to stop calling me that."

Robbie held up his fists. "What are you gonna do about it?"

"No fighting!"

Robbie turned to see his little girl standing on the stairs in her Dora pajamas, giving him the parental glare. "Uh, oh. Looks like we're busted."

"Speak for yourself," Jesse said, looking at Madison. "Maddie, I wasn't fighting. That was your silly dad."

She smiled, revealing two missing front teeth, and ran down the stairs and into Robbie's arms. "You are getting so big."

"I'm hungry."

"I know, baby girl. Let's get you something to eat." He turned to Jesse. "You're welcome to stay if you'd like. We're having dinosaur chicken nuggets and macaroni."

Jesse put a hand to his stomach. "Dinosaur nuggets! Those are my favorite. But only if I get to carry the princess upstairs." Robbie set her down and she walked over to Jesse. He placed one hand behind his back and held out his other to her and then bowed. She placed her tiny hand in his and did a princess curtsy. Then she climbed into his arms and Robbie just watched as he carried her upstairs to the apartment.

It was moments like these, when his little girl was absolutely happy, that he knew that Felicia would be proud. He looked up and smiled. "I miss you, baby."

Chapter Four

Sarah

Sarah opened the store at 9:00 a.m. sharp, something she had done every Saturday for the past three years, except for the occasional holiday closing. It was part of a routine that she had grown to depend on. She knew which flowers needed watering and which ones needed trimming, and she looked forward to the shipment that arrived at ten o'clock every day. Sarah loved her flower shop and knew how blessed she was to have it, especially now that everything else in her life was falling apart.

Rachael walked in through the back door. "What's up, boss?"

"The usual. We have some orders over there that need filled if you wanted to get started on them."

Rachael smiled. "I'll take care of them." She threw on an apron and picked up the stack of order tickets sitting on the counter. "Wow, this is a busy day."

Sarah finished watering the display roses. "There you go, babies. I bet you were thirsty."

"Excuse me?"

"No, not you." Sarah said to Rachel, setting the bucket of water on the floor. "I was talking to the roses."

"Ah," Rachael said, still looking at the tickets. "I'm sure they enjoy that."

"They do. You should try it."

"That's okay. I prefer humans." She splayed the tickets on the counter in little piles, organizing her workload. When Rachael had told Sarah that she wanted to help at the flower shop three years ago, Sarah thought that there was no way it would last. Rachael didn't exactly have the patience for flowers. Or for customers. Rachael was an acquired taste. "Besides, I'm not sure if I'd like what the flowers would say if they could talk back."

"If they did, they'd probably tell you about who stopped in yesterday." Sarah tried hard not to smile.

"Oh yeah?" Rachael studied her face. "Who's that?"

Sarah felt a smile forming across her face.

"Sarah Ramsey, I know that look. You better spill it now." Rachael walked around the counter and over to Sarah.

"Jesse."

"Jesse who?

"Really?" Sarah shot her an are-you-kidding-me look. "Jesse Malone."

Rachael brought her hand to her mouth and her eyes grew large. "Are you serious? I thought he lived in New York, working on becoming an architect or something like that."

"So did I. But he walked into the store yesterday. He and his fiancée."

"What!?" Rachael's eyes narrowed. "He had the nerve to show up here with his fiancée?"

"I don't think he knew that I worked here."

"You don't work here, Sarah. You own the place."

"You know what I mean." Sarah waved her off. "I don't think he knew. They want us to do the flower arrangements for their wedding."

30

"I have to sit down." Rachael grabbed a nearby stool, the look on her face registering shock. "I don't know how you're still standing."

"What else am I supposed to do? I mean, I was just as shocked as you, but what could I do?"

"Throw 'em out. The both of them!"

Sarah picked up one of the roses and clipped the end. "He's done nothing wrong."

"What!?" Rachael shot back up. "How can you say that? You loved him. You—"

"Rachael, he did nothing wrong," she interrupted. "We were both young and stupid. And besides, it wasn't like I was exactly innocent either. I was engaged to Kevin when Jesse and I…"

"Did," Rachael held up quotation fingers, "*it*."

"Stop it."

"It's okay, Sarah. We're adults. We can say what '*it*' is now. In fact, I just did *it* the other day with George."

"George Mutt? The delivery guy?"

A mischievous smile formed on Rachael's face as she nodded.

"Oh my gosh, Rachael. You barely know the guy."

Rachael picked up one of the roses. "That's not true. I know he has a nice smile and that he works for United Express and—"

"And that he stutters every time you talk to him."

"That, too." Rachael grabbed a rose and held it up to her nose. "He's so cute."

Sarah shook her head. Some things never changed. Rachael often used her beauty to spin a web. And once a man had fallen prey to her charm and outgoing personality, she dumped him. Like a disposable camera.

"Besides, you never let your hair down. Someone's got to have fun around here. May as well be me." Rachael tossed the rose into place and then walked back over to the counter.

"I'm still married."

"Not because you want to be. I mean, you filed for divorce over a year ago. When is that thing going to be finalized anyway?"

Sarah let out a sigh. Ever since Kevin's law firm had fallen under investigation, he had been hesitant to finalize the divorce. As if holding on to their marriage would somehow make things better. But nothing could make what he had done better. She had listened to him when he told her that the plant nursery was a mistake and that that type of a job wasn't suited for a pregnant woman or a mother with a young child. She had listened to him again when he told her that buying this place was a money pit, so she had held off on signing the contract for a year. But when he hit her—that's when she stopped listening to him. "I haven't been able to get a hold of him the past few days. He isn't returning my phone calls."

"Did you try calling the bars? I'd start with the strip joints first."

Sarah glared at her.

"What? Just sayin' is all."

"I don't know what to do. Emma asks about him all the time. I think she's starting to worry."

Rachael grabbed a ticket and headed over to the vases. "Emma's a tough little girl."

"I know. I just hate to see the look on her face whenever he stands her up. Not that they were ever really that close to begin with, but she does care about him."

Rachael grabbed a red vase and walked back over to Sarah. "Things happen for a reason." She placed a hand on her shoulder. "And right now you need to get this divorce finalized so that you and Emma can get on with life."

"I know."

"So, in the meantime, what are you going to do about Jesse the Jerk Malone?"

Sarah looked back at the bright red roses. "I have no idea."

Chapter Five

Jesse

A week had passed since Jesse had seen Sarah. Although he fought hard to push thoughts of her out of his mind, it was a fight he rarely won. He buried himself deeper into his work as a way of keeping himself distracted from the memories of her.

Going into work early and staying late seemed to help keep him focused. And since the Drake renovation bid was on the line, the extra hours at work were just what he needed. It was a twenty-million-dollar renovation that would span the course of a year. Not only would it bring in more money than four jobs combined, it would also put his small architectural firm on the map, opening the doors for even larger projects in the future.

"You've sure been putting in the hours," Nina observed.

"We're swamped," Jesse replied simply.

"We've been swamped ever since I started here, and I've never seen you put in this many hours. I just don't think it's good for you," she said, taking a seat at the front of his office. One of the things that Jesse liked about Nina was that she had the right amount of professionalism without forgetting the importance of a personal touch. He had no doubt that she would someday be running her own company.

"I'd like to have this project signed before going on my honeymoon."

"But that's why you brought me on, boss. I'm cheap labor and not afraid of working my butt off for you," she said, smiling.

"That's not why I hired you," he said. "Besides, you already do your fair share around here as it is. You should have a social life, too."

"I do. That's why I have my dog, Oscar," she said. "I tried the dating scene already and it didn't work out for me. It always ended the same. They'd complain that I worked too much. Or I wasn't ready for marriage. At least with Oscar, he never complains. He loves me the way I am."

Jesse laughed. He felt his cell phone vibrate and pulled it out of his pocket. He looked up at Nina. "It's Kate," he said.

"Tell her I said hi."

Jesse nodded and waited until Nina was out of the office before answering the phone.

"Hello."

"Hey, sweetie. How is your day going?"

"It's better now. What about you?"

"Not good. I'm on my way to the airport now."

"What? Where are you going?"

"New York. Nathan's threatening to quit and if I lose him, I'll lose half my client base over there. I have to fly out there and smooth things out a bit."

Beauty salon drama was the one thing he didn't like about her industry. Egos came in many shapes and sizes in the beauty profession, and they often didn't mix well with others. Jesse knew that it would be pointless to try to talk her out of going. When her mind was made up, there was no changing it.

"You there?"

Jesse let out a sigh. "Yeah, I'm here. I was hoping we could have dinner together tonight."

"I know, sweetie. But I won't be gone long. I should be back tomorrow night sometime."

"All right. Well, I'll miss you."

"I'll miss you, too," she said. "I do need you to do me a favor though."

"Sure. What is it?"

"I need you to drop a check off to Flowers of Chicago for me. Pay her half now and then we'll pay her the other half the day before the wedding," Kate said.

"What?"

"I'm sorry. I'm just in a hurry. This was the only flight I could get on such short notice, otherwise I'd stop by and pay her myself." She paused as if waiting for a reply, but Jesse said nothing. "Besides, you two are old friends. Maybe you can negotiate a better deal."

"I have a lot of work here. I don't know if I'll make it to the florist in time."

"Pretty please? Your old girlfriend's shop is one of the best in Chicago, and I don't want to lose out. I'll make it up to you."

"Hey! What's with the girlfriend jab?"

"I'm just giving you a hard time, sweetie. That's what a fianceé does when mysterious women appear from her lover's past."

"Funny girl. Okay. I'll do it," he said.

"Thank you. You're the best. And don't work too late. I love you, sweetie."

"Love you, too."

***

When Jesse got to the flower shop, he stood on the sidewalk trying to think of what he'd say if Sarah was there. He felt like an idiot. Like an awkward teenager who didn't know how to talk to a girl. He placed his hand on the door handle and took a deep breath before opening it.

The store looked empty of customers. It was just after 7:00 p.m., and he figured that most of Chicago probably had better things to do at that time than buy flowers. He walked up to the checkout counter and looked around. The store appeared to be just as empty of employees as it did of customers. "Hello?" he shouted to the back. "Anyone here?"

He listened carefully and heard some commotion in the back. Shortly afterward, the saloon-style door swung open and a woman walked through. Not Sarah, but someone else he recognized from his past. Sarah's friend, Rachael.

"Rachael? It's been a long time."

She just stared at him.

"It's me, Jesse."

"Oh," she said, continuing forward. "I remember now." She didn't exactly look happy to see him. In fact, just the opposite. "What brings you here?"

"Well, I was here a few days ago and—"

"That's what I heard," she interrupted. Then she crossed her arms and glared at him as if he had just done something bad to her.

"Is there something wrong?"

"No. I'm just waiting for you to tell me why you're here."

"Okay," he said, feeling a bit confused. "I just need to make a down payment on the flowers for my wedding."

"Yeah, I also heard that you were getting married now. What a lucky girl she must be." Sarcasm was plain in her voice.

"Excuse me?"

"Jesse Malone, I don't know what you're up to. But you need to listen to me. Sarah is—"

"Right here."

Rachael turned to find Sarah standing behind her.

"I can handle this, Rachael."

"Are you sure?"

Sarah nodded and Rachael went through the door leading to the back room, but not before glaring at Jesse one last time.

"Well, she sure hasn't lost her charm."

"That's Rachael for you."

"I remember her being a little...forward, but I don't remember her being that hostile."

"She's just protective is all."

"Protective of what? I'm just here to settle a debt."

"What did you say?" Sarah's face went pale as if she had seen a ghost.

"For the flowers." Jesse pointed to a picture of flowers on the wall. "I came to settle the payment for the wedding flowers. Kate said that I needed to make a down payment in order to reserve you guys."

"Oh, yes. The wedding arrangement." She pulled out a book from beneath the counter and began flipping through the pages. "If I remember correctly, you chose the Simply Beautiful arrangement." Her fingers slid down the pages.

"Sarah?"

"Yes," she answered without looking up.

"Is everything okay?"

"There it is, Simply Beautiful." Her fingers flew across the cash register as she calculated his total and then printed out a receipt. "Here you go. This is half the amount due in order to book the event. Second half due the day before the wedding."

Jesse noticed that she hadn't answered his question. Surely she'd heard him, but her lack of response had been just as much of an answer as if she had responded.

Jesse pulled out his checkbook and made out a check for the amount on the receipt. He tore it out and handed it to Sarah. She reached for the check, but he didn't let go. "Is something wrong?"

With the check still in both of their hands, she smiled. Then he released it. "No. I believe that you two have selected the perfect package for your wedding. I will call…Kate in a few days to finalize the plans."

"Sounds good." He quickly scanned the shop until his eyes settled back on Sarah. "Do you mind if I ask you a question?"

She didn't answer right away, making Jesse think he should just get out of there.

"Never mind," he said, turning toward the door.

"Sure," she said at the same time.

He turned back to her. "What ever happened to the greenhouse and the plant nursery?"

Sarah shook her head slightly. "It just didn't work out. After my father passed away, I realized that it was more of his dream than mine, and so I...I sold the land and the greenhouse and decided to open this place instead."

"Well, life certainly has been good to you. This place is beautiful."

"Thank you. I really can't complain," she responded, this time with a smile. "And you, too. This is the second time I've seen you and both times you've worn a suit."

He looked down at his clothes. "It's a necessary part of the job, I'm afraid. I'm an architect. I have a small firm over on East Ontario Street."

"Wow," she said. "That's impressive. You've made your dreams come true."

"Like I said, it's a small firm, but we're looking at a few bigger prospects with the hopes of expanding. But there's a lot of good competition in this city."

"I'm happy for you. I know your family must be proud."

Jesse noticed something different in her eyes. Almost like a guard had been let down, enough for him to see the old Sarah. The one he had fallen in love with all those years ago.

"Kate seems wonderful."

"She really is. I'm lucky to have her."

"You both are lucky."

Jesse placed his hand on the door. "Well, I should probably be going now."

"It was good seeing you," she said.

"Good seeing you." He pushed open the door and took a step out.

"Wait!"

He paused and reentered the shop. "Yes?"

"You forgot your receipt," she said, holding it up.

"Oh, yeah." He reached for the receipt and in that tiny exchange, something happened. He couldn't tell if it was her smile, the smell of her perfume, or the touch of her hand, but a spark of electricity shot through his body, barely noticeable, yet very much there. She pulled her hand back and stepped away from him.

"It was nice seeing you, Jesse."

"Same here." Jesse noticed her finger again, still barren of a ring. He knew it was time to leave, but his feet wouldn't move. He wanted to apologize for standing her up that day at the coffee shop. He wanted to tell her that he *had been* there. That he had had every intention of finding her later and explaining that, in order to keep Robbie out of jail, he had to agree to not show up at the coffee shop. It was the only way Kevin would drop the charges on his brother. And everything would have worked out except that Kevin showed up at the coffee shop instead and got down on one knee. The next thing Jesse saw was Sarah sliding Kevin's ring on her finger, making it official. What did he say? How could she accept the ring, after what they had just shared…after all they had been through together?

But the words never came. Instead, Jesse asked, "What do you think about grabbing a quick bite to eat next week? I don't work far from here. We could get something to eat and catch up a bit. You know, as old friends." And maybe he'd get the opportunity to set things straight once and for all and to apologize for not being there for her.

Sarah's smile faded as she stared at him. The uncomfortable silence had Jesse wishing he could withdraw the question.

Their eyes locked for a moment. Then a faint smile formed on her face, seemingly forced. "I'm pretty busy," she said. "But it was good seeing you today."

"All right then." As the store's door closed behind him, so did the door of closure. He had never meant to hurt Sarah, but it was clear now that he had. He looked down at the receipt in his hand, a reminder of why he had stopped by in the first place and a reminder of the woman he completely adored. Robbie was right. Kate was the one for him, and he was determined to see it through. No matter what.

Chapter Six

Sarah

The dryer's buzzer went off, notifying Sarah that her last load of laundry was ready. She set her book on the nightstand next to her bed and checked the time. Although it read 10:04 p.m., it felt a lot later than that.

It had been a typical day, one that consisted of getting Emma ready for school, opening and running the shop, helping her daughter with her homework, fixing dinner, watching two episodes of Phineas and Ferb, and reading Emma a bedtime story. Once Emma was asleep, Sarah began doing the laundry and straightening up their apartment. The day-to-day duties kept her life busy and organized. After her marriage fell apart, she'd grown to embrace this routine, and to depend on it.

On most nights she settled into her bed with a good book and a glass of wine, but fate had a different plan for her tonight. Ever since Jesse Malone had wandered back into her life, she had found it difficult to get him out of her mind.

After finishing the laundry she decided to give routine another shot. She poured a glass of red wine and headed back to bed for a few chapters before falling asleep. She'd gotten through an entire page when she realized that she couldn't remember anything that she had just read. Jesse's big blue eyes and crooked smile had penetrated her mind once again, making it impossible to focus on anything else.

So, she set her book down and called the one person she knew would be awake at this hour.

"Hello," Rachael said.

"It's me, Sarah."

"Yeah, I know. Why do you think I answered it at this time of night? What's going on?"

"Nothing. Just wanted to tell you that the Henderson wedding is this weekend, so we have to make sure we order the roses tomorrow."

"I already did."

"You did? That's great."

"Sarah, come on. We've been best friends for more than ten years. I know when something's bothering you. Why don't you just spill it and let me know what's on your mind."

Rachael did have a tendency to cut to the chase. Sarah said nothing at first. After all, how silly was it to be talking about a guy she hadn't seen in over six years. A guy who was getting married to someone else. And it wasn't like she was exactly available herself. Kevin had yet to sign off on the divorce papers. "Jesse came into the store today."

"I know, I was there when he showed up. It took everything I had not to punch him in that cute face of his."

Sarah remembered their encounter and how hostile Rachael had been to him. "He put down a deposit to book us for his wedding."

"Isn't that like a man? First he stands you up, breaking your heart. Then he leaves for New York without a word, only to show back up looking as handsome as ever and engaged to another woman. Why is it that the good looking guys are the jerks?"

Sarah didn't respond. Rachael had a way of rambling, most of which didn't make any sense at all.

"So, what else happened?"

"What do you mean?"

"You wouldn't have called me this late just to tell me that he stopped by to put in a stupid deposit for his stupid wedding. I mean, we are the best floral designers in all of Chicago, so it makes sense that they would hire us to do their wedding. Which means something else must have happened if you're calling me now. Did he kiss you?"

"No," Sarah protested. "Why would you ask that?"

"I don't know. It's my sick imagination, I guess. Besides, don't act like that would be an absurd thought. You're a hottie."

"Nothing like that happened. But he did ask me out to lunch."

"What!" Rachael shouted. Sarah had to pull the phone from her ear. "Shut up! Are you serious?"

"Yes. He said he thought it would be good for us to catch up," Sarah said.

"I'll bet he wants to *catch up*. He probably sees what a hot success you are and realizes what a doofus he was for breaking your heart, and now he wants to apologize."

"I doubt that," Sarah said. "He probably just wants to see how things are going. We were old friends."

"I'll say you were," Rachael said. "Friends with a flame big enough to set the city of Chicago on fire all over again."

"It's not like that. He's not like that. He wasn't flirtatious or anything." Sarah adjusted her pillow so she could lie down.

"So, what did you say?"

"I told him that I was busy."

Rachael didn't say anything.

"Rach, I don't know what to do. What do you think I should do?"

"Sarah, you already know what I think. I told you six years ago that you should call him up and give him a piece of your mind. And I've said the same thing every year since," Rachael reminded her.

"I know," Sarah said. "But he's engaged to be married, and she's a really nice person. I don't want to be the one…"

"Sarah, I love you, but you seriously have to stop being so nice all the time. He stood you up, remember? He's the one who broke your heart. He's the one who ignored your letter and worse yet, left town."

"I know. I get it. I'm just nervous. I fell in love with the guy, and when he left, I had to…"

"I know, Sarah. But if it were me, I'd talk to him once and for all."

"I just don't want anyone getting hurt."

"It's too late for that."

Sarah leaned over and turned off the light. "Maybe you're right, Rach," Sarah said, letting out a tired sigh.

"I know I am. Now get some sleep. Speaking of men, I have one of my own coming over in a few minutes."

"Oh Rach, not the exterminator again."

"Of course not. It's our delivery guy."

"Who? George?"

"Yep."

"Okay, now that's too much information. Have a good night."

"Trust me, I plan on it."

After hanging up the phone, Sarah turned over to lie on her side. Still no closer to an answer, she pulled the covers up to her chin. The moon shot light in through her window and onto the framed photograph of her dad on the nightstand.

"I've made a real mess out of things, Dad. I wish you were here now. You always knew what to do. And how to make me feel better."

Chapter Seven

Sarah

For the next few days, butterflies raged within Sarah's stomach every time the telephone rang. Ever since she had called Jesse to agree to lunch, she debated silently about whether or not she should actually follow through with it. She changed her mind from hour to hour and minute to minute. Things had changed so much since the last time she had seen him. Six years wasn't necessarily a long time, but for them it may as well have been a lifetime. And here she was now, with the nerves of a high school girl waiting for her crush to finally call her and tell her where and when they could meet. But this was different. He was different. Engaged. To a beautiful and apparently successful woman, from what she could gather from a simple Google search. She pushed it from her mind. It was irrelevant, she told herself. She didn't feel anything for Jesse. Not anymore. Not after what he had done to her six years ago. In fact, she wasn't sure if they could ever go back to being friends, and she definitely wasn't sure what to expect from this visit.

"Did he call yet?" Rachael asked.

"Who?"

"Don't act like you don't know who I'm talking about. Jesse 'Dreamy Eyes' Malone," Rachael said, batting her eyes.

"As a matter of fact, he hasn't. And it's probably for the best."

"You're no fun." Rachael snatched a stem of baby's breath from the fridge. "I've got it!" Her eyes grew large the way they always did when she schemed up an idea that would most likely end in disaster. "You should call him," she said.

"Wow, that sounds like a great idea," Sarah said, not bothering to hide the sarcasm. She finished cutting the stems off a dozen roses and then dropped them into a vase.

"I know, right?"

"I'm joking. It's actually one of the worst ideas you've ever had, and that's saying something." Rachael said nothing as she glared at Sarah. "I'm just messing with you," Sarah said. "But it *is* a bad idea. After all, I was the one who called him to tell him that I'd have lunch. The rest is up to him."

The front door opened and both Sarah and Rachael turned from their workbench to see their delivery man, George Mutt, walking through the door. His gray curly hair was a little too long for Sarah's taste, and although he had a cute smile, he was constantly clearing his throat, which drove her nuts.

"Hello, George," Rachael said flirtatiously.

"Hmm, hmm." George cleared his throat. "Hey there, Rach," he said as he disappeared into the back.

"You're shameless," Sarah whispered.

"Shameless?" Rachael wrapped a bouquet in brightly colored paper. "He may not look like much, but he has potential," Rachael said, smiling.

"I don't want to hear any details about Mutt's *potential*," Sarah said.

"Speaking of mutts, what ever happened to Kevin? Is he still missing?"

Sarah shook her head. "He called last night, wanting to see Emma."

"Are you serious? Where was he?"

"I didn't ask." She thought back to the last time she had seen him. His bloodshot eyes and the tequila that emitted from his breath like fire from a dragon had given her the creeps. He had wanted to see Emma then, too, but she told him to come back when he was sober. Something he rarely was these days. "He's had it rough lately."

"I bet he has. That's what happens when you try to rip off high-powered wealthy scumbags."

"Give him a break, Rachael." Sarah knew that if it hadn't been for her and the greenhouse project, Kevin would still be working for the district attorney's office. But he had traded a loan and a position at his father's law firm so he could finance the greenhouse. Something Sarah would have never agreed to if he'd asked her first. She knew that his father wanted nothing more than to get Kevin to work for him, something Kevin had been very much against. He enjoyed being on the good side of law, putting the bad guys away, instead of defending them.

"From what they are saying in the paper, someone else might be giving him a *break.*"

"Rachael!"

She threw her hands up in the air as if giving in to her. "Okay, okay. I'll stop now."

The telephone rang, startling Sarah and nearly causing her to cut off a finger. She stared at the phone, frozen with fear and anticipation.

"Well, are you going to get it?" Rachael asked.

The butterflies tickled the sides of her stomach into an ache. This is stupid, Sarah thought. Like it's going to be Jesse. She had to stop freaking out inside every time someone called.

She picked up the phone. "Flowers of Chicago, this is Sarah, how may I help you?"

"Hello, Sarah." Jesse's voice stirred the butterflies into a hurricane of fluttering.

"Oh, hi, Jesse," she said, looking over at Rachael. Rachael quickly dropped her scissors and ran over to Sarah, placing her ear right next to the phone.

"I know it's short notice, but would you be free for lunch today? I had a client cancel on me, and I thought this might be a good opportunity for us to grab a bite to eat and catch up."

"Today, well I..." Sarah stalled, thinking of any reason why she couldn't make it. Rachael was nodding vigorously as she mouthed the word yes. "I guess I can make it," she replied. "What time?"

"How about in an hour?"

"An hour?"

"Is that a bad time?" Jesse asked. Rachael shook her head and mouthed the word no.

"No, that should be fine," Sarah said.

"How does that pizzeria down the street from your shop sound?"

"A Slice of Heaven?"

"That's the one," Jesse replied.

"Sounds fine."

"Great," Jesse said. "I'll see you in an hour."

"Okay, see you then." Sarah hung up the phone.

"Now look who's shameless," Rachael said, slapping her on the shoulder.

***

When Sarah showed up at the pizzeria, she looked for a hostess when someone caught her eye. A handsome man wearing a suit and tie sat in a booth next to the window. Jesse Malone. A million memories and feelings came rushing back like a wave of heat.

He looked the same and yet so different. His brown hair was no longer long and wild but was instead cut neatly above his ears with parts sticking up at the front, making him look like a young politician. She hated how attractive she still found him. Stay focused, she reminded herself. She had come here for a reason, for an understanding, and to let Jesse know what he'd been missing all these years, and she couldn't waver now. She took a deep breath and headed toward him.

He stood when he saw her and gestured to the seat in front of him.

"Hey there," he said, waiting for her to sit.

"Hi, sorry I'm late," she said, taking a seat across from him in the booth.

He looked at his watch. "Only a few minutes."

"Have you been here long?"

"Nope. I just got here." Jesse took his seat across from her. "Have you ever eaten here before?"

"Yeah, a few times. Their pizza is delicious."

"I think it's one of the best pizza joints in the city," Jesse said. "What kind of pizza do you like?"

Sarah opened the menu in front of her and scanned the lunch specials. "I'm a huge pepperoni and sausage lover."

"Me, too."

A tall waitress with short, spiky blonde hair stopped by and pulled out a pen and pad of paper. "Can I get you two somethin' to drink?" she asked.

"I'll take an iced tea," Sarah said.

"I'll take a Coke."

The waitress didn't bother writing down their drink order. "Do you still need a minute to order?" she asked them.

"I think we know. Right?" Jesse asked, looking at Sarah.

"Yeah, you go ahead," she responded.

"We'll take a large pepperoni and sausage lover's pizza," Jesse said, looking up at the waitress.

This time she took some notes on her pad. "All right, I'll be right back with your drinks."

The restaurant seemed fairly empty for lunch hour, leaving the two of them with plenty of privacy. Sarah put down the menu and collected her nerves before looking Jesse in the eye.

He shot her that crooked smile that used to melt her heart.

"What is it?" she asked.

"I just can't believe it," he said. "I can't believe that I'm sitting here having lunch with Sarah Ramsey."

"I have a hard time believing it myself."

"Well, you look great," he said. "Time has had absolutely no effect on you."

Sarah felt her cheeks flush. "Thank you," she said. "You look the same, too. Except your hair is a little shorter."

Jesse ran a hand through his hair. The same way he used to when it was long. "Yeah, I thought it was time for a change."

"Well, what have you been up to?" she asked.

He sat back in his seat and let out a sigh. "A lot," he said, as if not sure where to begin. "I ended up going to New York for grad school, Columbia actually."

"Wow, Columbia, that's impressive," she said. "Who took over the pet shop? Your Aunt Sherry?"

"No. She was never into the day-to-day details of the operations. Robbie took over. He has some help though. He hired a guy right out of the military. Ricky Everlee."

"That's great. How is Robbie?"

The waitress stopped by and dropped off their drinks. "He's doing well." He removed his straw from the wrapper. "When he got locked up that last time, my Aunt Sherry went in and talked some sense into him. I guess it worked since he couldn't exactly get away from her. We were lucky that most of the charges were dropped. He did a few years of probation and gave up boxing. But he's been straight for years now."

"Good for him. I always liked Robbie," Sarah said taking a drink. "Once I stopped being scared of him, of course."

"You'd barely recognize him anymore. He's really settled down. He and Ricky opened a second location, which keeps them plenty busy."

Sarah had a hard time picturing the tattooed, muscular guy with a shaved head as a business owner. Although she did remember how nice and funny he had been around her. "And how's Aunt Sherry?"

Jesse looked down at his drink. His smile faded and he slowly twirled the condensation-covered glass with his fingers. "She passed away a few years ago," he said.

"Oh, I'm sorry to hear that." She knew that since Jesse had lost his mom at the age of twelve, his Aunt Sherry had been the closest thing to a mom he'd had.

"She passed away in her sleep," Jesse said. "Robbie's the one who found her. Her little terrier, Bailey, was curled up next to her. That dog never left her side."

"He was such a cutie."

"Bailey died about four weeks later. He wouldn't eat or drink anything. We tried everything, and nothing worked. We took him to the veterinarian where he spent his last few days."

"That's so sad," Sarah said. "I wish I'd known. I'd like to have attended her service."

"You would have liked it. There were lots of flowers."

"I bet it was beautiful."

"What about you?" Jesse asked, changing the subject.

"What about me?" She looked down at her drink, trying to avoid the spotlight and suddenly remembering why she had agreed to lunch in the first place.

Just then, the waitress showed up and placed their pizza and two plates on the table in front of them. "You two enjoy. I'll be back to check on you in a few."

"It smells good," Sarah said.

Jesse grabbed the silver spatula. "You want this piece here?" he asked, pointing to a big slice.

"That's fine," she said, holding out her plate.

After serving himself a piece, they both took a bite. "Wow, this is so good," Jesse said.

Sarah nodded. The warm tomato sauce and melted cheese blended to a perfect bite of pizza. "It's definitely one of the best in Chicago."

"So," Jesse paused to take a drink. "What have you been up to?" he asked again.

"Not as much as you," she said, pausing to think about what she was going to tell him. She had a feeling he would want to hear about her relationship with Kevin, which was exactly what she didn't want to go into. It wasn't like it had a happy ending. And she hated the look people gave her when she told them that she had filed for divorce. It was as if she'd told them that she had a terminal illness. "After I sold the greenhouse and the plant nursery, I kind of floated around for about a year, trying to figure out what I wanted to do next."

"I know you mentioned it briefly at the store the other day, but I'm still confused as to why you sold it. You loved that place."

"I don't know...after my father died, I guess I lost interest." When Sarah was completely honest with herself, she knew that this was partially true. But the entire truth had been something she chose not to think about.

"That surprises me."

"What does?"

"It's just that I remember the look on your face when you were at the nursery. You looked at that huge empty landscape with such...knowing, as if you knew exactly how it would be someday. You seemed happy there."

"I guess things change," she said, taking a drink.

"Yeah...I guess."

The pause in conversation gave her the perfect window of opportunity to ask Jesse the question she had wanted to ask for the past six years. The nerves in her stomach felt like rocks weighing her down in the seat, making it difficult to move, to speak. She set her slice of pizza on the plate and wiped her hands on a napkin. Then she took a deep breath. "I—"

Jesse spoke at the same time. "Sarah, there's a reason why I asked you to lunch. And it wasn't just because I wanted to catch up either." He paused and looked out the window. Sarah could see the busy sidewalk of people passing by in Jesse's large blue eyes. "I wanted to clear some things up." He turned back to Sarah. "Some things that have been bothering me for the past six years."

A brief wave of relief along with continued nervousness filled Sarah as she waited for him to say what he had to say. Yes, there was a reason he had asked her to lunch and a reason why she had finally accepted. And this was it.

"Sarah, do you mind? I need to use the restroom." Jesse didn't wait for a response before getting up and walking away, leaving Sarah with a stomach full of knots and a slice of pizza she could no longer eat.

Chapter Eight

Jesse

Jesse walked into the tiny bathroom and went straight to the sink. He looked into the mirror and then turned on the water, letting it run through his fingers before splashing a handful onto his face. "Come on, man. You can do this."

"Sometimes you just have to talk to him to get him to work. I'm not judging you, man."

Jesse turned to the only stall in the bathroom and saw a pair of pants sitting on a pair of tennis shoes. Oh great, he thought. What a day. He had choked when it came to finally apologizing to Sarah after all these years and now some strange dude in the bathroom thought he was talking to his member. "It's not what you think," Jesse responded.

"Like I said. I'm not judging you."

"I can't believe this is happening," Jesse murmured.

"It happens to all of us eventually."

Jesse pumped the paper towel lever a half dozen times before tearing off a piece and wiping his face. He tossed it into the trash and took one last look in the mirror. "You can do this."

"Sure you can," the man agreed. Jesse just shook his head and walked out.

Before returning to his table, he watched as Sarah stared out the window. Time hadn't changed her a bit. If it had, it had only made her more beautiful. Her long blonde hair fell past her shoulders. Her smooth skin looked like beige silk. His heart raced at the sight of her.

"Sarah, sorry for that."

She turned and flashed a smile. "It's okay."

Jesse took his seat and pushed his slice of pizza to the side. "There's something I need to tell you."

"What is it?"

He took a drink of his Coke. The burning carbonation and sweet syrup ran down his throat as he thought of the best way to tell her what he had wanted to tell her for the past six years. "I did go to New York to work on my master's degree, but I also felt like I needed a new beginning for myself."

"What brought you back to Chicago?"

"Robbie and Madison. And Kate's family is here, too."

"Oh, I see." Sarah sounded a bit disappointed. "So, did you and Kate know each other before New York?"

Jesse nodded. "We were friends here in Chicago before I moved to New York. She moved out to New York about a year after I did to open a salon. We continued our friendship and then became roommates."

"She seems wonderful."

"Kate's great," he agreed. "I mean, we couldn't be any more different. She comes from a wealthy family, and I come from...well you know, New Haven, Indiana. Not exactly a booming metropolis."

"Hey, small towns aren't all bad. I'm from there, too. You may not be able to get pizza like this there, but they have some of the best broasted chicken you can find anywhere."

"I'll give you that," Jesse chuckled. "Anyway, we don't have a lot in common, but there's something about that girl that just makes me smile inside."

"That's nice." Sarah took a sip of her drink.

"What about you?" Jesse asked.

"What about me?"

"Did you ever get married?"

Sarah sat back in her seat and crossed her arms. "Yes."

"To Kevin?"

She nodded. "It didn't work out though."

"I'm sorry to hear that." Jesse could tell by her body language and lack of words that she was uncomfortable with the conversation.

"It's okay. Things were good at first, but then…I don't know, they just changed. And we couldn't find a way to get things back on track." Sarah paused and then asked, "Who's Madison?"

"Excuse me?"

"You said you moved back here for Robbie and Madison."

"Oh, Maddie. She's my rambunctious niece."

Sarah's face lit up. "Robbie's daughter?"

Jesse nodded. "She's adorable. She looks just like her mother, Felicia."

"I didn't realize Robbie had gotten married."

"He didn't." Jesse ran a hand through his hair. "They were going to get married. Right after Maddie was born. But Felicia died giving birth."

"Oh, that's so sad. Poor Robbie. So, he's been raising his little girl on his own."

"Yeah. And he's the best dad, I swear. I never would have guessed it myself, but he's like a giant teddy bear whenever she's around. I've never seen him more at peace."

Jesse could see tears well in Sarah's eyes. He grabbed a tissue and handed it to her. "I'm sorry. I'm not usually like this." She dabbed her eyes and looked at Jesse who had just been staring at her. "What? Is it my makeup? Is it smeared? I must look a mess."

"Not at all." In fact, he had never seen a woman look more beautiful. Something he chose to keep to himself. "Sarah?"

"Yes?"

"There's something I have to tell you."

"What is it, Jesse?"

"You remember the plan we had of meeting at the coffee shop? The day after we had spent the night together?"

"Caffeine Corner."

"That's the place."

"I remember. What about it?"

"I was there that day."

"You were? I was there, and I didn't see you."

"I know you were." Jesse leaned forward. "I saw from beneath a tree across the street. You were sitting at the same table where we had those delicious chocolate chip cookies."

"I don't understand." Confusion filled her face.

"After you left the pet shop, the morning after we...well, the day before we were supposed to meet, Kevin came by. He told me that if I agreed not to meet you that day, he'd convince the district attorney's office to drop Robbie's charges so that he wouldn't have to go to jail for breaking into the electronics store. And after everything Robbie had done for me, I had to help him. Besides, he's my brother, Sarah."

Sarah's eyes narrowed and she looked down at her crumpled napkin. "So, Kevin told you that he'd help Robbie if you didn't show up at the coffee shop?"

"Yes. But I had planned on finding you later, after Robbie had been released, so that I could explain everything to you. But..."

"But you were there, and you saw Kevin get down on his knee and slide a ring on my finger?" A defeated look filled her eyes.

Jesse nodded. "I wanted to be there that day."

Sarah didn't say anything. Her eyes were as unreadable as a book without words.

"I'm sorry, Sarah."

A few moments of uncomfortable silence passed. "So, that's it?"

"Is what it?"

"That's what you have been wanting to tell me for the past six years? That you stood me up to free your brother?"

"Yes. And like I said, I couldn't let him just rot in prison. Not after all he had done for me."

"I would have done the same thing," she said. "I just can't..." Her words fell off.

"If you understand, then why do you sound so upset?"

She looked at him, her eyes brimming with tears. "I can't believe that after six years, that's all you have to say."

"Sarah, I'm trying to apologize. What else do you want from me?"

A tear rolled down her cheek and fell from her face. "I think it would be a good idea to find someone else to handle your flowers, Jesse. I'm not the right person for the job. I'll send you a check refunding your down payment." She stood up and grabbed her purse.

"Wait! What did I do? All I wanted to do was apologize. I've thought of that day at least a thousand times, and I—"

"Goodbye, Jesse." She turned and walked out of the pizzeria. Jesse watched as she opened the door and the wind blew her hair back, hoping she'd at least give him one look back. But she never did.

Chapter Nine

Jesse

Jesse sat in his office, thinking about his lunch with Sarah. He played their conversation over and over in his mind, trying to figure out what he could have said to offend her. Everything had seemed fine until he apologized. Was she that upset that he had stood her up to free Robbie? That couldn't be right. After all, she said that she would have done the same thing. Then what happened? The closure he had hoped for with Sarah had ended in disaster. And how on earth was he going to explain to Kate that he had lost their florist? Her wedding was a day she'd been dreaming of ever since she was a little girl.

He stared at his computer screen and tried to focus on work, but it was no use. The Drake bid was due in less than two weeks and he had so much left to do. The harder he tried to focus, the more he thought about Sarah and the tear that had slid down her cheek after he had apologized to her.

"Are you okay?" Nina asked from his office doorway, holding an armful of files.

"Huh?" he said, looking up at her. "Yeah, I'm fine."

"You don't look like it," she said. "You look like you just lost your dog."

"I don't have a dog."

"I know. It's just an expression," she said. "Are you sure you're okay? Maybe you should get out of here for the rest of the day. Go take Kate out to a movie or something."

"Yeah," he said, turning back to his screen. "I think I will get out of here for the day. I need to swing by and check on the Old Town job anyway."

"I already did that this morning."

"You did?"

"Yep. On my way to work. Everything looks good. They're actually ahead of schedule," she said. "Never underestimate the power of doughnuts and fresh coffee in the morning. The guys will probably do just about anything for me now," she said, smiling.

"Did I ever tell you that you're good?"

"Not nearly enough. Now get out of here," she said, continuing down the hall.

"Thank you," he called after her.

Jesse looked at his watch and saw that it was 4:30 p.m. He grabbed his jacket, walked out, and jumped into a taxi. "Where to?" the cab driver asked.

Jesse thought for a second. "Flowers of Chicago on Michigan Avenue." He couldn't go home and tell Kate that they needed a new florist for the wedding. Besides, he couldn't stand how upset he had made Sarah. He had to make this right.

After ten minutes of honking and shouting, the cab driver pulled to a stop in front of the flower shop. Jesse paid and stepped out. A cool breeze splashed across his face, causing him to pause. He stood in front of the glass doors of the store. Then he grabbed the handle and took a deep breath. He walked inside and saw Sarah standing in front of the large display of roses. She wore a green apron with images of various flowers splayed across it.

"Sarah," he said.

She turned around and her jaw dropped when she saw him. "Jesse? What are you doing here?"

"Is this a bad time?"

Just then, the swinging door in the back flew open and a little girl came running out. "Mommy! Mommy!" she shouted as she ran to Sarah and threw her tiny arms around her.

Sarah hugged her tightly, glanced at Jesse, and then looked down at the little girl.

The little girl's large blue eyes and straight brown hair reminded Jesse of someone. Someone he had seen in black and white photos taken before he was ever born. He stood frozen as his heart quickened.

"Emma," Sarah said. "Can you please go to the back with Grandma?"

Jesse took a step back, bumping into a display of teddy bears.

"But I have to tell you something," the little girl insisted.

"Okay, hon, but it's going to have to wait. Mommy's at work and she needs to help this customer." She gestured toward Jesse, and the little girl looked at him with those large blue eyes, and Jesse knew without a doubt. He had a daughter.

Chapter Ten

Sarah

Sarah watched Emma disappear beyond the swinging door and braced herself before turning back to Jesse. He was gone, the door to the shop swinging shut.

She followed him outside and shouted, "Jesse!"

He turned around but said nothing.

"I'm sorry," she said, shaking her head.

"Is that…is she…?" He pointed into the store.

Sarah nodded. "She's your daughter, Jess."

"What? How did this…"

"You know how this happened. Why are you acting so surprised?"

Jesse took a few steps forward, and Sarah could see the fire and anger within his eyes. "For six years, you knew. You knew that she was my daughter and you kept her from me." He slammed his hands into his chest. "I have a daughter and you kept her from me!"

"Don't put this on me. I showed up to tell you, but you were gone. Gone without a word. So, I left you a note. I left it for you, explaining everything. And all these years went by and you didn't say anything, you didn't do anything. Not even a birthday card or a letter explaining why you wanted nothing to do with her."

"What are you talking about? I never got a letter, Sarah. I got nothing. Not even an email for crying out loud. Don't you think I had a right to know?"

"What do you mean you didn't get a letter? I left it for Robbie. A week after you left for New York. He said that he'd give it to you."

"Robbie? No…" He paused as if trying to remember. Then he looked down and ran a hand through his hair.

"Jesse, I'm sorry you had to find out this way." She took a step closer and placed a hand on his arm.

He jerked it away. "Don't touch me." His voice displayed the anger his eyes had been showing. "You should have…"

"What? I should have what?"

"You should have said something! You should have called me! SOMETHING! ANYTHING!" He pointed to the store. "I have a little girl, and I had no idea. I lost six years and now what am I supposed to do?"

A large lump formed in the back of Sarah's throat. What had she done? All these years she'd thought Jesse wanted nothing to do with their little girl. When he had stood her up at the coffee shop, she thought he didn't want to be with her, and she could live with that. But when he hadn't answered her letter, she thought he had turned his back on his little girl, something she'd struggled with for six years. But she was wrong. Wrong about everything. The lump grew larger, making it difficult for her to breathe. "Jesse, I'm so sorry."

"It's too late, Sarah." He took a step closer and lowered his voice. "You stole six years from my life." He pointed a finger at her. "I'll never forgive you for that." Then he turned and walked away.

"Jesse! Wait!" she pleaded. But he didn't stop. Didn't turn around. Her tears streamed down. "Jesse, I'm sorry." She stood on the sidewalk, crying, lonely, unable to stop the darkness that covered her. "What have I done?"

Chapter Eleven

Robbie

There were still two hours left before closing, and Robbie knew they'd drag. He had taken inventory, set up the next day's deliveries, and fed all of the animals. He decided to let Ricky take over the register while he went upstairs to feed Madison. Although he knew that Mrs. Winters, their nanny, would be able to do it for him, he just craved some time with his little angel.

He had gotten to the first step when he heard the brass bell hanging above the entrance ring. Ricky said, "What's up, Jesse?"

Robbie smiled and turned around. "Wow, twice in less than two weeks. So, to what do I owe this honor?"

Jesse ignored their questions, heading straight for Robbie. "Why didn't you tell me?" he demanded, anger evident in his voice.

"Tell you what, little bro?" Before Robbie could take a step back, Jesse had his shirt in both hands. He pushed him into the wall behind him. "What's your problem?"

Jesse continued to hold on to Robbie's shirt. "You're my problem, Robbie."

Robbie's back and chest ached from the collision. He felt anger shooting through his veins and his hands tightened to fists. "Listen, Jess, you'd better take your hands off me before you push a button on me that you don't want to push."

Jesse slammed him against the wall again. "You should have told me!" Jesse shouted.

"Stop it!" Madison shouted from the top of the stairs. She tore down the stairs and started pulling at Jesse. "Let go of my daddy. You're hurting him."

Robbie spoke. "Jesse, this is the last time I'm telling you." He lowered his voice to a whisper. "I don't know what you're talking about, but I'm about two seconds from tossing your ass out of here. You're out of line, little brother."

Jesse let go and released a deep breath as if he'd been holding it ever since he'd walked into the store. Robbie felt his racing heart slow to a normal pulse. Jesse turned and put his back against the wall. Robbie knelt down to Madison and gave her a hug. Her thin arms squeezed around his neck as if she planned to never let go again. "It's okay, baby girl. Uncle Jesse's just upset about something. It's going to be okay now."

Tears filled her green eyes. "Are you sure, Daddy?"

Robbie nodded. "Yes, baby. Why don't you go upstairs to Mrs. Winters, and I'll be up in a few minutes to make you some dinner?"

She turned to Jesse and then looked down as if he'd just broken her heart before turning away to climb the stairs. Robbie waited until she was out of sight before turning to Jesse. "What the hell has gotten into you, man?"

"You never gave me Sarah's letter!"

"What are you talkin' about?"

"The letter Sarah gave you." Jesse poked a finger into Robbie's chest. "*You* told her that you'd give it to me, and you never did."

Robbie crossed his arms. "What letter?"

"The one she gave you six years ago. Right after I left for New York."

Robbie thought back to the day he had said goodbye to Jesse. Standing with Felicia under his arm, he'd watched him drive away in the taxi. Robbie remembered it as one of the saddest and best days of his life. The day that he officially took over the pet shop and his entire life changed. No more hanging out with thugs, no more breaking into houses and stores stealing merchandise and peddling it on the streets of Chicago. "Jess, I have no idea what you're talkin' about. The last time I saw Sarah was when I asked her to visit me in lockup. When I told her—" And then it hit him like a wrecking ball crashing into a wall. "I'm so sorry, man. She did stop by. A long time ago. She asked to speak with you, but you'd already left for New York, so she handed me a letter to give to you."

Jesse's eyes narrowed. "What did you do with the letter, Robbie?"

"Listen, man. You had just been through the ringer with that girl. You finally went away to finish your schooling, and I knew that that girl would only get into your head."

"Robbie! Where's the letter?"

"I threw it away." Robbie watched as Jesse's head dropped. "I did it to protect you, man." Jesse's back slid down the wall until he was sitting on the ground. "What's the big deal? I mean, look at you." Robbie gestured to Jesse. "You graduated. You started your own architecture company. And you're about to marry one of the most beautiful women in all of Chicago."

"I wouldn't be too sure about that."

"Why would you say that? What does a letter have to do with anything?"

Jesse looked up at Robbie. "Because I have a little girl."

"What are you talkin' about?"

"Exactly what I said. Sarah came to talk to me that day because she was pregnant with my baby."

"Are you serious?"

Jesse nodded.

Robbie's back slid down the wall until he was sitting next to Jesse. "Oh man, I am so sorry. I had no idea."

"I know you didn't. I just wish—" Jesse stopped himself. "There's no point in wishing anything now. It is what it is."

"So, did she tell you that you have a daughter?"

"She didn't have to. I saw her with my own two eyes."

Robbie nudged him with his elbow. "Well, how do you know if she's...you know?"

Jesse gave Robbie an are-you-kidding-me look. "I saw her. She looks exactly like Mom did in those black and white photos when she was a kid. And her name is Emma. She has Mom's name, Robbie. She's definitely mine."

"No way." Robbie shook his head. "This is...so crazy." He turned to Jesse and immediately felt the weight of guilt like a giant rock in his gut. "I feel so shitty for not giving you that letter, man."

"Forget about it. There's nothing we can do about it now."

"So, what you are going to do?"

Jesse looked up at the cage of puppies playing. "I don't know. But there is something that I have to fix right now."

Chapter Twelve

Jesse

Madison's eyes lit up when she saw the rows of ice cream flavors behind the glass display. "So, what's it going to be?" Jesse asked. "Vanilla, chocolate chip mint with sprinkles, or how about cotton-candy flavored?"

She scanned each flavor before zeroing in on the chocolate brownie ice cream. Then she pointed and said, "I want that one."

"That's a good choice," said Joe, the owner of Moo Town Ice Cream. He brought a silver scooper out of a tub of water and put two giant scoops on a sugar cone before handing it to Madison. "Two scoops of chocolate brownie for the princess." Then he turned to Jesse. "What about you?"

"Give me the usual, Joe." Jesse had frequented this place when he worked at the pet shop. Being just a short block away, it made for a tempting and convenient trip, especially on a warm summer day.

Joe went to work on filling a waffle cone for Jesse. "Haven't seen you around in a long time, Jesse."

"I've been busy."

"You," Joe pointed to Robbie. "I see you all the time."

Jesse looked at the tiny belly forming just above Robbie's belt. "I can see that."

Robbie rubbed his stomach. "Hey, wait until you have kids, and see how long that six pack of yours hangs around."

Jesse's shoulders dropped and he looked away. "Oh, man. I'm sorry. I wasn't thinkin'," Robbie said quietly.

"It's all right."

"Can I go sit in front of the fishes?"

Jesse knelt down. "Hey, Maddie. I'm very sorry for being so mean earlier. I'm not usually like that. I just had a really bad day today. Although I know that's no excuse."

"I know, Uncle Jesse. Sometimes I get mad, too, and throw Mr. Rabbit on the ground. Daddy always tells me to calm down. He says that you should never lose your temper. Whatever that means."

Jesse chuckled. "Your daddy's a smart man. Now can I have a hug?" She wrapped her free arm around Jesse, careful not to spill her ice cream, and then kissed him on the cheek.

"Now can I go sit by the fishes?"

"That's up to your dad."

Robbie looked down and nodded. "Go ahead."

Madison walked over to the round table in front of the large aquarium, one of the attractions Joe had installed to keep the kids coming back for more ice cream.

"You bribed her with ice cream," Robbie said.

"Yeah, well, you've got to stick with what works."

"Ice cream definitely works."

Jesse watched as her pink elephant slippers bounced with each step. "She's so much…"

"Like her mother," Robbie finished Jesse's sentence.

Jesse nodded.

"I know. Every day she does something or looks at me in a way that reminds me more and more of Felicia. I love it, but..." Robbie grabbed a few napkins from the dispenser. "But it also makes it difficult to move on, you know?"

"I can only imagine. Speaking of moving on, when are you going to get out there and start dating again?"

Joe handed Jesse his cone. "It's good seeing you again, Jesse."

Jesse held up his cone. "Good seeing you, Joe." They walked over to a booth where they could keep an eye on Madison. She licked the top of the cone, as if completely oblivious to the melted ice cream falling down the sides.

Robbie stared at his vanilla cone before answering. "I tried dating a few times."

Jesse smiled. "How did that go?"

Robbie shook his head. "Not well. It's tough, you know. I have the shop to run. Plus, we've opened the second location since you left. Then there's Maddie." He looked over at her and a proud smile filled his face. "She definitely keeps me busy."

"I bet. But don't you think she'd like to have someone else in her life, too?"

"It's not that simple." Robbie took a bite of his ice cream. "Dating as a single parent is a lot like interviewing someone for a job. It puts a lot of pressure on me as the parent, but also the other person. Especially when the other person is looking for more of a honeymoon type of atmosphere when dating. It's more difficult to do when you have a curfew because the babysitter's waiting for you to get home or if your kid gets sick and you have to cancel altogether. A lot of people don't get it."

Jesse watched Madison as she stared at the fish and tapped the glass with her finger. She did remind him of Felicia. He couldn't help but wonder if Robbie also found it difficult to move on because of how strongly he had loved her. She had been the one who pulled Robbie out of the gutter and crime he had fallen into. She was the one who had taught him that the man he had been wasn't the man he had to be. Something Jesse had tried for years to do and failed. "I can see how it would be hard."

Robbie followed Jesse's line of sight, and his face lit up again as he watched Madison make fish faces at the fish. A small part of Jesse envied that. He couldn't imagine the sense of joy Robbie felt being a father. He wondered if he'd ever be able to feel the same way about Emma. A pang of guilt filled his gut, causing him to lose his appetite.

Robbie placed his hand on Jesse's shoulder. "Listen, little brother, everything's going to be all right. I know it is."

"I just don't know what to do. I've lost six years with her. She doesn't even know who I am, let alone that I'm her father. And what if she's been raised to believe that Kevin is her dad? Then what? I can't exactly step in and take the role now. That would be too damaging for her."

"Slow down." Robbie gave his shoulder a squeeze. "Remember that day when our father showed up?"

Jesse remembered his father's bloody fist pounding into his mother's flesh as if he'd been tenderizing meat. That had been the day that changed everything for Jesse and Robbie. The day Jesse killed his father and Robbie ended up taking the heat for it. Sure it was self-defense and didn't lead to jail time, but in a way it had. The years of name-calling that Robbie suffered after that. The label he had been branded with as the Murdering Malone from New Haven, Indiana, stuck with him all the way to Chicago. Their Aunt Sherry and Uncle August tried their best to shelter them from the pain of their past, but Robbie hadn't been able to escape. A price he paid for Jesse, and the debt Jesse repaid the day he chose to stand Sarah up so that Kevin would get the charges against Robbie dropped. "How can I forget?"

"We lost our mother that day. And then we ended up living with our aunt and uncle."

"So, what does that have to do with this situation?"

"Didn't they feel like our mother and father?"

Jesse looked down at his melting ice cream, wondering where Robbie was taking this. "I guess."

"It wasn't because they conceived us. And it wasn't because they took us in either. It was because they loved us like we were their sons. It was love that created that bond. Nothing else."

Jesse took a bite of his ice cream as Robbie's words sank in. Maybe he could do this. Maybe he could find a way to be Emma's father. Jesse's phone rang. He pulled it out, looked at the caller ID, and then silenced it.

"Who was that?"

"Kate."

"Aren't you going to answer it?"

Jesse shook his head. "And say what? Hey Kate, you know the florist you hired for our wedding? Well, we did know each other a little better than I'd led on before. In fact, we actually have a little girl together. So, how was your day?"

Robbie laughed. "Okay, so it won't be easy."

"Easy? It will be anything but."

"You are going to have to tell her the truth eventually. I mean, she's going to wonder who this little girl is that you have hanging out at your apartment every other weekend."

Jesse let out a sigh. "I know. I know." Then he turned to Robbie. "When did you get to be so wise?"

"I had a pretty smart little brother who kept me on my toes." Then he punched Jesse on the arm. "That's for earlier."

The top scoop of Jesse's ice cream cone fell onto the tiled floor. "Hey!"

"Sorry," Robbie said, walking away with his cone still intact.

Jesse watched as he took a seat next to Madison. She smiled and pointed to the fish inside the aquarium, showing him the ones that were her favorite. Ice cream began dripping from her cone onto the table, creating a pool of chocolate. Robbie tried wiping it up, but it continued to drip. For the first time in Jesse's life, he thought about what life would be like as a father. And he liked it. Then his phone rang again.

Chapter Thirteen

Sarah

Sarah checked her watch for the twelfth time in the past twenty minutes.

"I'm sure they're just stuck in traffic. You know how bad Chicago traffic is at this time." Rachael's words of encouragement did little to ease Sarah's nerves. This was the first time in a month that Kevin had exercised any visitation with Emma. And with everything going on with his job, she worried for Emma's safety. Kevin hadn't been the most predictable person when it came to a crisis.

"I'm sure everything's okay. I bet they stopped somewhere for dinner." She checked her cell phone to see if she had a text message, but none popped up on the display.

"Have you heard from Jesse?"

"Not since the other night when he…"

Rachael filled a red vase with roses and water and set it in the fridge. "So, let me get this straight. He stood you up that day at the coffee shop six years ago because scumbag Kevin…oops, I mean scumbag Kevin, your fiancé, said he'd drop the charges against Jesse's brother, Robbie, if Jesse was a no-show at the coffee shop? Then Kevin shows up instead, telling you this story about how Jesse told him that he knew Kevin was the right man for you and that Kevin should meet you at the coffee shop instead of him and finally, he presents you with a ring to confirm your engagement?"

Sarah nodded.

"And then you marry the creep."

"Thanks a lot."

"Sorry." Rachael flashed a smile. "Then you marry the scumbag." She paused as if waiting for Sarah to reply. "You find out shortly after that you're pregnant, but when the doctor tells you the probable date of conception, you realize it's Jesse's baby, so you get up the nerve to see him and he's not there. His brother tells you that he'd moved to New York the week before. You write a letter and give it to his oaf of a brother, who promises to give it to Jesse, but apparently Jesse never got it?"

"Yep. That about sums it up."

Rachael puts a finger to her chin. "Does this mean that I have to stop hating Jesse 'Dreamy Eyes' Malone?"

"I never told you that you should hate him to begin with." Sarah opened the register and started to count out the cash. "You should have seen the look on his face, Rach. He hates me."

"Do you blame the man? I mean, he just found out that he has a beautiful little girl who he hasn't ever met. I'd be a little pissed off, too."

"I know. I just wish—" Sarah paused when she heard the sound of the entrance door open. She held her breath, hoping to see Emma walk through with a bouncing ponytail and a huge smile on her face, but instead she saw Kevin making a grand entrance. "Where's Emma?" Sarah's heart fell to her stomach.

"Relax. She's just dragging her feet."

Emma came walking in behind Kevin, her head down and her backpack looking more like a boat anchor weighing her down. Sarah's heart broke for her. "Hey, honey. How was your day?"

Emma looked up at Sarah and a bright smile filled her face. Her entire demeanor seemed lighter once she had her mother in sight. She dropped her backpack and ran over to Sarah, nearly tackling her with a hug. "Oh, I missed you so much, sweetheart," Sarah said as she squeezed her little prize.

"I missed you, Mommy," she whispered.

"Well, that's the most excitement I've seen from her all day." Kevin's voice penetrated the warm moment she was having with her daughter.

Sarah pulled away from Emma's embrace, leaving her hands on the sides of her daughter's face as she looked her in the eyes. "Emma, why don't you and Rach go to the back and get started on your homework."

"Okay, Mommy." She walked over to Rachael who already had her hand out ready to catch Emma's.

"Hey there, squirt. So, tell me all about that boy, Kyle, from your class I've been hearing about." Leave it to Rachael to make every conversation about boys.

Sarah stood up and straightened her apron. "Thanks for bringing her by."

"No problem. I think we need to discuss her attitude though."

"What are you talking about?"

"Didn't you notice? She acted as if someone had stolen her favorite stuffed animal."

Her favorite stuffed animal was a giraffe she had named Butter Cup. Something Sarah was sure that Kevin wouldn't know if asked. "I think she seemed fine. Maybe she's just a little tired."

"Then maybe her mother should get her to bed at a decent time."

His smug comment caused her skin to crawl. But baring her teeth now was exactly what he wanted from her, so she bit her tongue instead. "So, what did you guys do?"

Kevin walked over to an exhibit against the wall where she displayed her top sellers. "I had some things to do at the office. Things have been crazy at work."

She imagined that he was underplaying it a bit. The papers had been having a field day with his case. In fact, there were talks of having him disbarred. She pictured Emma, sitting in a stiff leather chair and playing Barbie by herself. It was bad enough that she rarely saw her father, but now, when he finally does show up, to totally ignore her... just like he had ignored Sarah when they were married. She was so riled, but, as much as she wanted to tell him how she felt, she knew that this was neither the time nor place. "Is that whole mess about finished?" she asked.

He turned slowly and walked toward her. His slick black hair held streaks of gray, something that had started shortly after he took the position with his father's firm. Long hours and mountains of stress had taken a toll on him, but he always wore a neatly pressed suit and kept his face shaven. Image was everything to him. *It's the first thing people see.* One of the many sayings he had adopted from his father. The closer he got, the more her stomach tightened. "Are you worried about me, Sarah?"

Sarah took another step back until she felt the counter behind her, but that didn't stop Kevin from coming closer. "I'm not worried. I was just curious."

Kevin stopped with twelve inches of separation between them. "It's very sweet, but you don't need to worry about me." He put his hands on his chest. "I'm not going anywhere." He leaned in closer, placing his face mere inches from hers. He closed his eyes and drew in a deep whiff. "You smell so delicious. At first I thought it was the flowers, but I should have known. You always smell enchanting."

The insidious smell of rum emitted from his breath, causing her stomach to flip. She held her breath and peered over his shoulder. His shiny silver Lexus sat on the curb in front of the store. "You son-of-a-bitch. You've been drinking. And you drove *my* daughter out here." She leaned forward, causing him to take a few steps back. "If you ever do that again, I swear…"

"You swear what, Sarah." Kevin put his finger in her face. "That's what I thought. If you ever tell me what to do with *our* daughter, that will be the last thing you do."

"Is that so, Mr. Big Shot?" Rachael stood just inside the swinging back door. Sarah must not have heard her through the rage shooting through her body.

Kevin held out his hands and revealed his perfect white teeth. "Hey, Rach. It's always a pleasure to see you."

"I wish I could say the same." She walked over to the other side of the counter and stood between Sarah and Kevin. "If you ever threaten my friend again," she said, holding up a pair of stainless steel scissors, "I'm going to cut off your balls and feed them to my dog."

Kevin's smile faded. He straightened his tie and looked at Sarah. "I'll see you next week."

Sarah didn't respond. Instead, she waited for him to walk out of the shop before she let out a deep breath, not realizing she'd been holding it. She leaned back against the counter, letting it support her weight.

"Can you believe him?" Rachael turned toward Sarah.

"I'm scared, Rach. He's never threatened me before. And…" Sarah looked down at her trembling hands.

"And what?"

"I don't know. I just get this feeling that maybe he's been…following me."

"You think he's spying on you?"

The thought sent chills down Sarah's back. She rubbed her arms and nodded.

"Why do you believe he's following you?"

"Well, I'm not sure if he really is or not. I just feel like I keep seeing him. You know, from a distance. But when I try to get a closer look, he's gone."

"Wow!" Rachael brought her hand to her mouth. "That's just plain creepy. You should look into some protection."

"What kind of protection?"

"I don't know. Pepper spray? A handsome bodyguard?" she asked, winking at Sarah.

"Stop it. I don't want either. I just want him to sign those damn divorce papers."

Rachael placed her hand on Sarah's shoulder. "I hate to bring this up now, but as long as he thinks he's Emma's father, he will never be out of your life."

Sarah looked down. "I don't know what to do." When Jesse hadn't shown up at the coffee shop the day after their night together at the willow tree and hadn't responded to her letter, she assumed he didn't want anything to do with her or Emma. If she'd told Kevin the truth back then about Emma being Jesse's daughter, he would have left her, which at the time was the last thing she wanted. Sarah had hoped to give her daughter the perfect family. But she had failed. Life with Kevin had been anything but perfect. "How do I tell Emma that the man she's been calling Dad her entire life really isn't? I know they don't have the best relationship, mainly due to all the hours he's worked since she's been born, but he's still the only dad she's known."

"I don't know what to tell you, Sarah. I'm afraid there's no easy way out of this one. But you do have to get him to sign those papers regardless. That will at least give you some separation from the bastard."

Sarah nodded. Rachael leaned against the counter next to her. She nudged Sarah's arm. "Besides, you don't need a bodyguard when I'm around. I'm great when it comes to dealing with jerks."

Sarah chuckled. "Yes, you are. But you do realize that you don't have a dog, right?"

Rachael held up her scissors. "I was on a roll."

Chapter Fourteen

Jesse

More than a week had passed since Jesse had found out about Emma. He could barely eat or sleep, and when he was with Kate, he said very little, afraid of giving anything away. After all, when she agreed to marry him and become his wife, she didn't exactly agree to being a mother to a daughter he never knew. Not to mention the whole issue about where they were going to get their wedding flowers now, assuming there would even be a wedding. So, he focused on the one thing he had left: work.

Jesse started going in earlier, often beating Nina to the office, which was something he had seldom done before. He also worked well into the evening hours. If Kate called and asked when he was coming home, he simply told her that he had the Drake deadline and it couldn't be helped. At least that was partially true. With a rapidly approaching deadline, he had to make sure every detail had been accounted for. And for the most part, it worked.

"Hey, boss. I'm heading home. You want me to lock up?"

"That's all right. I'll be here a little while longer."

Nina walked into his office with her briefcase and umbrella in hand. "What's gotten into you lately?"

"What do you mean?"

"You're beating me to work, which means you have to be getting in before six o'clock in the morning. And you're staying well into the night on most days. Is everything okay?"

Jesse looked up from his blueprints. "Yes. I just have so much to get done. We have two more days to get that bid in, and I want to make sure we've thought of everything."

Nina turned one of the blueprints around and stared at it. "It's going to be fine, you know? This is some of your best work. They'd be stupid not to pick you."

"That's nice of you to say. But it's not just about price on this one. They're looking for someone who not only understands the hotel's rich history, but the city as well. They're going to be looking hard at the tiniest of details."

"Which is exactly why you've got this one. I'm telling you, no one loves or understands this city as well as you do. You should go home and get some rest. Spend some time with that lovely fiancée of yours. I'm sure she's missing you by now."

Luckily, Kate had had a few emergencies of her own at her hair salons that had kept her at the office later than usual. "I doubt that. She's been just as busy as I have lately. She'll probably be working pretty late today."

"Actually, I was hoping that you'd take me out to dinner tonight."

Nina smiled and stepped to the side, revealing Kate, who'd been standing behind her. Relief and nervousness battled within Jesse. A week had passed since he had had a good conversation with her. He missed her, but at the same time, he worried that his behavior would send off alarms within her, potentially exposing the secret he'd been carrying all week. And he knew that he wasn't prepared to get into all of that now. Not with the Drake bid and the wedding just around the corner. Not to mention he still didn't know what to do about Emma. He'd concluded that he wanted more than anything to be in her life, but where would he start? There was no manual on how to handle situations like this.

"I'll let you two be alone. See you in the morning, boss." Nina waved to them both and then walked out.

"What do you say? Can you do dinner tonight?"

Jesse looked down at his blueprints and then at his computer screen. Then he looked up at Kate. Her tired brown eyes told him that she needed this dinner just as much as he did. "Sure. It sounds good."

***

Jesse stared across the table at Kate as she scanned the menu, something she often did every time they ate at Buca's, even though she always got the same dish.

"What are you looking at?" she asked.

"The most beautiful woman in this restaurant."

Her full lips formed into the perfect smile. "Mr. Malone, you are one smooth operator, aren't you?"

"No. I'm just having a hard time finding anything on this menu that sounds as good as you."

She laughed loudly at that, drawing attention from some of the surrounding tables. "Now that was terrible."

"Come on. I've been working on that one all week."

"It's a good thing you're a talented architect."

"And why's that?"

"With lines like those, you wouldn't make a very good pickup artist."

"Is that so? Because I'm pretty sure that I picked you up."

She placed a napkin on her lap. "I'm pretty sure I was the one who picked you up."

Jesse sat back in his chair. "No. I was the one who wooed you, remember?"

She looked up and tapped her chin, feigning thought. "I'm convinced that I am the one who swept you off of your feet."

Jesse remembered the day he had planned a romantic dinner in their tiny apartment. The day he had finished his classes and wanted nothing more than to celebrate with her. The same day she had come home with an engagement ring from Nate, the guy she'd been dating for a few months. Jesse had been so busy with school that he had no idea how serious it had become. And knowing what it was like to lose someone he loved for fear of telling her, he was bound and determined not to let that happen again. "You don't remember, do you?" he said.

"Remember what? Me living with you as your roommate for two years while pining for you the entire time?"

"I don't remember any pining going on. But I do remember you coming home with that engagement ring."

Kate shot him a what-are-you-talking-about look. "I don't..." Then the light bulb clicked on. "Oh yeah, Nate. He was a sweet guy, but he wasn't the right man for me."

"So, does that mean I am?"

She moved her hands to the center of the table. He met her halfway and grabbed her hands, squeezing them until a smile formed on her face. "You are definitely the man for me, Jesse Malone. And I can't wait to marry you."

The pit returned to his stomach, a reminder of what he had yet to tell her. He let go of her hands and picked up his menu. "I need to figure out what I want."

The waiter showed up a minute later and took their orders before relieving them of their menus and heading back to the kitchen. "I'm starving," Jesse said, rubbing his stomach.

Kate cocked her head to the side. "So, when are you going to tell me what's going on with you?"

"What are you talking about?"

"I've noticed, Jesse. For the past week you've been…somewhere else. At first I thought it was work, but work has never caused you to withdraw like this. I've tried to be patient, but with the wedding a few weeks away, I'm starting to get nervous."

"Nothing's going on. I've just been busy."

She gave him a studied look. "No. There's something else. Now spill it."

Jesse sat forward, placing his elbows on the table, and rubbed his hands together. "I've just been worried about losing this bid. It would mean so much for our small company. There's a lot riding on it."

She sat back and crossed her arms. "All right. Have it your way. But if you're having cold feet, Jesse Malone, you'd better tell me."

"I'm not having cold feet. The opposite, actually. I can't wait to marry you."

"Really?"

"Really. You're beautiful, smart, funny, well, sort of funny."

She feigned a sad face. "I thought you loved my sense of humor."

"I was kidding. I do love it." Jesse had to admit. She had changed quite a bit in the time that he'd known her, but who didn't from the age of twenty to twenty-six? Her confidence showed in her work and in the way she carried herself. It had always been one of her more attractive qualities.

She leaned forward and grabbed Jesse's hands. "Listen, I know something's bothering you, and if don't want to tell me, just promise me one thing."

"What's that?"

"Please, just talk to someone."

The words she planted in his mind took hold, and he knew in that moment what he should do. Something so obvious and so close that he simply couldn't see it before.

"I'm fine." He brought her hands to his lips and kissed her fingers. "I can't wait to marry you."

Chapter Fifteen

Robbie

Robbie looked down at Maddie, who had crossed her arms in front of her and refused to look at him. "This isn't fun."

"That's not true, Maddie. Look at all of the flowers inside. Aren't they so beautiful? Just like you."

She shook her head, causing her brown curls to bounce around her shoulders. "I want to go to the park."

Robbie looked at the store and then back at his unhappy little girl. "Let's make a deal. You come in here with me while I talk to the lady inside, and then I'll take you to the park."

Her frown transformed into a smile and she held out a business hand. "Promise?"

Her tiny hand felt like a puppy's paw within his giant grasp. "Promise," he said, shaking her hand. She must have gotten this tactical side from her mother, he thought. He wished he'd had half of her intelligence when he was her age. "Now can we go inside?"

She nodded, sending her curls bouncing again.

Robbie turned toward the door just as it opened and a man with slick black hair and a business suit bounced off of Robbie. "Hey, watch it!" the man said, straightening up as he fixed his tie.

"I'm sorry. I didn't see you coming out," Robbie explained.

The man smiled, revealing a set of perfectly white teeth. Robbie's eyes narrowed, as he tried to remember where he'd seen this guy before. "Don't I know you?"

The man scanned Robbie from head to toe. "I highly doubt that." Then he walked away.

Robbie felt a tug at his shirt. "Daddy?"

"Yeah, baby girl?"

"Do you know that man?"

He watched the man walk with confidence down the sidewalk before getting into a silver Lexus parked on the curb. "I'm not sure." Then he looked back down at Maddie. "He wasn't a very nice man, was he?"

She shook her head in agreement.

They walked into the store and an overwhelming floral fragrance filled his nose, as if someone had bottled spring and kept it locked inside this quaint little store. Robbie didn't know the first thing about flowers, but judging by the prices on the displays, he figured this place was high-end. The type of store he and Felicia probably wouldn't have used had they had the chance to get married. She had good taste, but good financial sense. After all, flowers don't last.

Robbie noticed a woman bent over near a display, and he walked over to her. Broken glass and water surrounded her. "Are you okay?"

She looked up with red eyes and tear-soaked cheeks. "I'll be with you in a minute."

"Sarah? Is that you?"

She looked up again, her hands full of the shards of glass she'd been collecting off the floor. "Robbie?"

"That's right. Jesse's brother."

She stood up and wiped her cheeks with her free hand. "It's good to see you."

"Yeah, it's…good to see you." He motioned to the mess on the ground. "What's all this?"

"Oh, it's nothing. I knocked over some vases. Just clumsy."

"Mommy! Mommy!" A little girl with straight brown hair in pigtails came walking through a set of swinging doors. "What happened?" Robbie's heart stopped beating when he saw her large blue eyes. Jesse was right. The spitting image of his mother in the old photographs she used to show them.

"Nothing, baby. Stay clear of this mess." She placed her hands on the little girl's shoulders and walked her off to the side. "It was an accident—"

"Emma."

The little girl looked up at Robbie. "How do you know my name?"

"I used to know your mom."

"I've never seen you before."

A dog with yellow and white fur put its nose in Maddie's hand. "Daddy, look. They have a dog."

"His name's Willow," Emma said, walking over to Maddie. Her hand sank into his soft fur, and she rubbed the back of his neck. "He's really soft. Do you want to pet him?"

Madison looked up at Robbie. "Go ahead. But let him sniff your hand first."

Willow sniffed the tips of her fingers and wagged his tail. Then he ran his tongue across her hand. "That means he likes you." Emma rubbed the back of his neck with both hands. "That's a good boy."

"Em, why don't you take your new friend to the back and show her where Willow likes to sleep and the toys he plays with."

Emma reached a hand out to Madison. "Come on. I'll show you."

Madison checked with Robbie again. "It's okay. I'll come get you in a few minutes."

Robbie watched as they walked hand-in-hand through the swinging doors, Willow trotting behind them.

"I can't believe it. She looks so much like our mother."

Sarah smiled. "Your little girl looks like you."

"Madison has her mother's eyes, brains, and good looks. She has my nose and stubbornness." He ran a hand over his closely shaven head. "I'm just glad she didn't get my hair."

Sarah laughed. "It's not that bad. It's a bit longer than the last time I saw you."

"Well, I've been growing it out for the past six years."

She let out another laugh, this time louder. "It's good seeing you, Robbie."

He looked down at the mess. "So, what happened here? Doesn't look like any accident I've ever seen."

The smiled faded from her lips. "I'm just clumsy is all."

"I see." He remembered the guy who had slammed into him on his way out. "That must be going around."

"What's that?"

"Oh, nothing." He now knew who Mr. Teeth was. Kevin, the guy he had almost laid out six years ago when he walked his smug smile into his pet shop looking for Jesse. "I actually didn't come here for flowers."

"You don't say." She placed her hands on her waist and shifted her weight to her back leg. "I had you pegged for a roses guy."

"Yeah, if they're plastic and only require a little dustin' every now and then." He looked around. "Although, this is a beautiful setup you have here."

"I'm glad you like it." She set the glass on a counter and bent down to gather more. Robbie knelt down next to her and started gathering some of the larger shards. "You don't have to do that. I'm pretty sure you didn't come here to clean up my messes either."

"No. Actually, I'm here to clean up my mess."

She looked up at Robbie with a curious expression. "What are you talking about?"

"I'm sorry, Sarah."

"For what?"

"You remember that day you stopped by the shop lookin' for Jesse? And then you handed me that letter to give to him?"

"Yes." She let out a sigh as if he'd opened an old wound.

"Well, I never gave it to him. I just...he was finally getting his life together. Finally doing something for himself, instead of for someone else. And I just wanted..."

"To protect him," she whispered softly. One corner of her lips formed a half smile. "I get it. I know what you two have been through together. And I remember how ferociously you protect each other. And here I was, coming back into his life, complicating it once again."

"But I know now that you weren't trying to do that. I know now. I just wish that I had known then. I wish I could go back and change things. The last thing I wanted to do was rob my little brother of more than five years of his daughter's life."

She placed a hand on his shoulder. "It's okay. I think I was doing the same thing."

"What do you mean?"

"I immediately assumed that he wanted nothing to do with me, or Emma. But deep down inside, I knew better. Jesse would never abandon his responsibility. His heart's too big." She stood up and then set the glass on the counter. "I think the reason I didn't try to contact him after that was because I knew he'd quit school and run back to Chicago. And I guess I was afraid to be the one who did that to him. Besides," she brushed her hands over the counter, "I had already married Kevin, and I think a part of me was afraid of what would have happened if Kevin ever found out. That's the part that I'm going to have to live with. I just hope that Jesse can find a way to forgive me someday."

Robbie grabbed Sarah's hand. "If I know my brother, he already has. Just be patient. He'll come around."

Chapter Sixteen

Jesse

Jesse stared at his computer screen while tapping his pen on his desk. He looked at the clock, disappointed that only nine minutes had passed since the last time he'd checked it. The board was out now on the Drake's renovation deal, and between that deal and everything that had transpired over the last few days, Jesse found it hard to focus on his other projects.

Nina stopped in the hall and leaned inside his office. "Hey, boss, they may not have a decision for a few days. You keep doing that, you'll wind up tapping a hole through your desk."

He looked down at his hand, not realizing he'd been doing that, and then stopped. "Sorry. I've got a lot on my mind lately."

"Well, don't worry about the Drake proposal. You've got that one."

"How can you be so sure?"

"Because you're the best and I saw your plans. They were brilliant."

"How many times do I have to tell you that flattery will not get you a day off?"

"And how many times do I have to tell you that I wouldn't take one if you offered it. Besides, you wouldn't know what to do if I weren't here."

There was a bit of truth in her sarcastic statement. She'd been with him now for two seasons and had taken the reins on many of his smaller projects, especially as he'd worked on this bid. He'd been so far removed from the action of it all that it'd take him a week just to reacclimatize. "Really think we've got a shot?"

"Absolutely. Is there anything else you need to get done? I've got everything covered here for now."

Jesse looked at his watch and then thought about what Kate had said at dinner the other night. *I know that something is bothering you. Promise me…that you'll talk to someone.* "Actually, if you don't mind, there is something that I need to do."

"Go for it."

"All right. If anyone calls looking for me, tell them that I'll be back later this afternoon."

"You got it."

Chapter Seventeen

Sarah

Sarah had finally finished putting away the new shipment of flowers when she heard the entrance door open, announcing the arrival of a new customer. "I'll be right with you." Out of the corner of her eye she saw Willow come tearing through the store, heading right for the customer. "Willow!" she shouted. "You're not supposed to be up here."

"That's all right. He and I go way back."

She saw Jesse crouch down with his hands cupping Willow's face as he rubbed behind his ears. She remembered the day Jesse had given her Willow, when he was just a hyper ball of fur. A puppy so tiny he'd fit inside both hands. It had been an unexpected surprise, kind of like Jesse's visit now.

"Hey, Jesse. It's good to see you."

He turned his gaze to Sarah for a moment. "It's good to see you, too."

"You sure about that, because the last time we talked, you didn't seem very happy with me."

Jesse let out a sigh and stood to face Sarah. "I know. And I'm sorry for that. It was a lot to take in, you know?"

"I know. I am glad that you're here now though."

"I can't believe how big he's gotten."

Sarah watched Willow's tail flip back and forth as Jesse bent back down and rubbed his floppy ears. Willow looked up and surprised Jesse with a kiss on his lips. "Hard to believe he was ever small enough to fit inside that tiny cage at the pet store with all those other pups."

"I know," Jesse said. "Robbie still has that same cage at the pet shop."

"Did Robbie tell you that he stopped by a few days ago?"

Jesse's eyes narrowed. "No. I don't suppose he was here buying flowers."

Sarah shook her head. "He came to apologize about the letter."

Jesse looked back at Willow. "Yeah. I was a little hard on him, I guess."

"He had his little girl, Madison, with him. She's adorable."

"She's his pride and joy. And she looks just like her mother."

"She and Emma really hit it off."

Jesse took a few steps closer. "Actually, she's why I'm here. I think we should talk."

"That's what I figured." Sarah tucked a few strands behind her ear. "When did you have in mind?"

"Now if you have time."

"Now?" Sarah turned to Rachael who had wandered over to the wall of flowers behind Jesse, pretending not to listen. When she saw Sarah look at her, she started dancing and mouthing the words "He is hot." Jesse turned to see what Sarah was staring at, and Rachael quickly ceased, but Sarah was pretty sure he had caught a few moments of the show. "Yes," she chuckled. "I can definitely talk now."

"We could walk over to Millennium Park across the street. Take a walk and get some fresh air."

"That sounds good." She saw Rachael doing the happy dance again and gestured for her to stop.

"I'll wait outside while you get your things." Jesse turned around, and Rachael nearly fell over trying to compose herself. She dropped a pen, picked it up, and walked casually past Jesse. "It's good to see you, Rachael."

"Back at ya, Jesse."

Sarah noticed her flushed red cheeks and laughed. She couldn't remember the last time she'd seen Rachael embarrassed.

After the door closed, Rachael said, "It should be illegal to be that good looking. It's not fair."

"Well, you're a beautiful girl."

"I know I'm beautiful. But guys just shouldn't be that pretty. It's not fair to us beautiful women to feel as though we have to compete with them."

"You are definitely original." Sarah grabbed her purse from behind the counter. "Are you sure that you're going to be okay here alone?"

"Of course I am. Now get out there with Mr. Hottie before he changes his mind."

"It's not like that. We're just going to discuss Emma. And where we should go from here."

"I'll tell you where you should go from here. Straight to his bedroom."

"Rachael!"

"Just sayin'."

Sarah walked over to the glass door entrance to look for Jesse. He sat on a bench seat facing the store with his elbows resting on his knees. He looked nervous. But who wouldn't be in a situation like this. For the past week and a half, she had tried to imagine what he must be going through right now. What kind of betrayal he might feel or any ill feelings he might harbor because of it. But Jesse was different. Jesse was…special. His heart was not only big, it was made of pure gold.

Sarah took a step outside and a breeze caught her hair, sending it whipping across her face. She walked over toward Jesse, pulling her hair out of her eyes, and froze. She saw someone standing beneath a tree in the park across the street. Kevin. She blinked, hoping it had only been her overactive imagination, but there he stood, leaning against the tree with both hands in his pockets. His eyes fixed on her like a lion ready to pounce on his prey. Her heart started to race. A traffic light turned from red to green, sending a steady stream of traffic and blocking her view of him. She looked at Jesse.

"Are you okay? You don't look so good."

She turned back to the tree and waited for the line of cars and buses to pass. She tried to focus in the brief moments between passing cars but it was no use. And when the traffic finally disappeared, so had Kevin.

Chapter Eighteen

Jesse

Jesse noticed Sarah look over her shoulders a few times, as if expecting to see something. "Are you okay?" Jesse asked. "We can always do this another time."

"No," she said, looking over her shoulder one last time. "I thought I..." She shook her head. "I thought I recognized someone, but...I must be seeing things." She smiled at him. "I must be working too much. Just ignore my craziness."

They walked across the street to Millennium Park. The temperature had been unseasonably cool for mid September, but it was still too hot for his suit. "It's a gorgeous day," he said, removing his jacket.

Sarah looked up at the blue sky. "I doubt we'll see any rain today."

When they reached the paved walkway, they instinctively slowed their pace. Jesse had no idea where to start. The nerves building in his stomach reminded him of the day he and Sarah had had their first kiss beneath the willow tree. They were twelve and life had been simpler. Sure they had their problems at home. Jesse, Robbie, and his mom lived in a dilapidated trailer, hiding from their father, an abusive drunk. And Sarah lived across the creek in Whispering Meadows, where the houses were large and the people had more money than they could spend. At least that's how Jesse saw it back then. But all the money in the world couldn't save Sarah's family from the tragic loss of her little brother, Henry. The loss that ultimately tore apart their family. But when they were standing beneath that willow tree, everything always seemed to make sense.

Sarah still hadn't said anything, as if waiting for Jesse to speak first. And neither would look the other one in the eyes.

"You should have told me," Jesse said finally, breaking the silence.

"I know. I know," she said. "I think I was scared."

"Scared of what?"

"I don't know exactly. I mean, here I was, married and pregnant with another man's baby. And then you were off living your dream in New York. I think a part of me was afraid of holding you back, like everyone else in your life had done."

What she said made sense. It didn't make things any less painful or easier, but at least he had a better understanding of the situation they were in. Jesse turned and looked up at the tall oak trees in the park. "Do you remember when we were kids and we would hang out in the willow tree?"

"Yes."

"Sometimes I wish I could have one of those days back."

"Me, too."

"But we can't," he said, turning around. He paused for a moment and let out a sigh. "Sarah?"

"Yes?"

"Please tell me about her."

Sarah tucked a strand of curly blonde hair behind her ear. "She's five. Her birthday is February 9th. She loves unicorns and Littlest Pet Shop dolls." She paused and looked down at the sidewalk.

"From the brief moment that I saw her, she looked good. She seems healthy."

"Except for the occasional sinus infection, she's a perfectly healthy, happy, and curious little girl. She has your straight brown hair and your big blue eyes, which she's used against me many times." A slight smile formed on Sarah's face, as if she pictured her right then and there. "And that smile." She pointed at him. "Everyone says that she has my smile, but I know better. Every time she gives me that crooked smile, it melts my heart."

"I don't know what you're talking about."

Sarah pointed at Jesse's mouth. "You're doing it right now. I swear, when I look at you, it's like I'm seeing her."

"What kind of stuff does she like to do? Play with dolls? Play with her friends?"

"She likes collecting maps."

"Maps?"

"Yep. I have no idea where she gets that. But she has a drawer full of maps. From all over the place. She says that one day she wants to buy a huge boat and travel around the world." Jesse stopped walking and looked at Sarah.

"She's ambitious. I think she gets that from you." He thought he saw her cheeks flush before she turned away. The park had plenty of visitors. People taking advantage of the nice day.

"Emma loves this park," Sarah said, looking around. "We come here about once a week. She'll run up and down the grass and in and out of the trees."

"That sounds nice." He imagined them spending their Sundays here. Walking the paths and playing hide-and-go-seek, just before eating a picnic lunch.

"There's a bench over there." Sarah pointed to a stained wooden bench. "Would you mind if we sat for a moment? I wasn't exactly prepared for a walk in the park," she said, looking down at her shoes.

Jesse looked down at her polished high heels. "Sorry, I hadn't noticed."

"It's okay. I just need to sit for a moment," she said, taking a seat.

Jesse took a seat next to her and threw his jacket over the back of the bench. "So, how does Emma do in school?"

"Good," Sarah said. "She's not a straight-A student, but she applies herself and gets her fair share of them."

"What's her favorite subject?"

"She loves English, and science is her weakness. She likes reading okay, but loves singing in the choir."

Jesse looked behind them at the people across the street going about their busy days, each with their own story. "My mom used to sing."

"She did?"

Jesse nodded and laid his arm across the back of the bench. "We had this little radio that barely picked up two stations. Robbie had fashioned an antenna out of a wire hanger just to get those two. I remember Sundays, the only day my mother had off, she'd turn on the radio and sing as she did dishes and laundry. Her voice was so beautiful."

"That sounds nice. The thing about Emma that reminds me the most of you is her serious side."

"What's that supposed to mean? I'm not that serious."

"No, not at all," she said, her sarcasm obvious. "She has this intensity and depth that just doesn't seem normal for a kid her age. And I know she doesn't get that from me."

Jesse looked down and tried to think about what life would have been like raising a daughter. Teaching her how to fish, helping her with homework, and being there for her first steps. "I missed out on so much," he said.

Sarah turned to face him. "I'm sorry."

"Her first steps. First words."

"She was ten months old. And her first word was mama," she said, leaning in closer and placing her hand on his arm. Her touch was electric and sent tiny bolts shooting through his body. "I'm truly sorry," she said again.

Jesse looked into her crystal blue eyes. They danced as they reflected the sunlight, drawing him in just like they did when they were twelve and then again ten years later when they conceived Emma that magical night beneath the willow tree, after digging up her mother's ring in the time capsule. His heart sank to his stomach as he slowly leaned in to her. With his lips just a few inches from hers, an image of Kate flashed in his mind, and he backed off. "I can't do this," he said. "I love Kate now."

"I understand," she said, leaning back. "I'm sorry. I shouldn't have…It's just that…" She reached up and rubbed the side of his face. Then she leaned toward him and kissed him gently on the cheek. "I understand that we missed our chance. I had to let you go a long time ago, Jesse Malone. Emma was the one way that I was able to hold on to a piece of you. And I'm sorry I didn't try harder to have you in her life. I just hope you can forgive me some day." She brought her hand back down and said, "I should probably get back to work."

A cloud of confusion filled with mixed feelings created a hurricane of emotions within Jesse. He looked back toward the bustling pedestrians across the street. Then he saw someone who looked a lot like Kate, standing still amidst the river of people making their way down the sidewalk. His eyes narrowed to get a better look, and he realized that it was Kate, standing on the sidewalk across the street and staring right at him and Sarah, a horrified expression on her face.

"Kate!" Jesse shouted. But Kate took off running. He stood up and ran around the bench after her. She reached the end of the block but didn't stop, running straight into the intersecting street.

"Wait!" he shouted, but it was too late. A red SUV slammed on its brakes and Kate froze. The vehicle hit her, and she flew a few feet to the hard pavement, her limp body rolling down the street.

Jesse continued across the busy street, not paying any attention to the passing cars. The tires of a blue minivan squealed as it slid toward him. He slammed his hands on its hood as he side-stepped to avoid ending up beneath its tires.

His body went numb from adrenaline as he sprinted to Kate, who lay lifeless in the street. "Kate!" he shouted. When he reached her, blood covered the side of her face.

Jesse gently wiped the blood away from her face and shouted, "Someone call 9-1-1!" He rocked back and forth as tears rolled down his cheeks, falling onto Kate. "I'm so sorry, Kate. I'm so sorry."

Chapter Nineteen

Jesse

Jesse sat beside Kate, holding her hand while the EMTs did their job.

He closed his eyes and tried to block everything from his mind. The sound of sirens and EMTs calling out instructions faded until they were completely gone.

Then he slowly opened his eyes and looked at Kate's swollen and bloody face. Tears filled his eyes, blurring his vision. "Kate. If you can hear me, I'm so sorry. I never meant for this to happen."

The ambulance pulled up to the hospital and the back doors flew open in the emergency bay where a doctor stood ready. The two EMTs riding in the back jumped out and pulled Kate with them.

They wheeled the gurney through the halls while the EMTs filled the doctor in on Kate's situation. "Who's this?" the doctor asked them.

"It's her boyfriend."

"Fiancé," Jesse said, correcting him.

"Were you there when it happened?" the doctor asked.

"Yes." Guilt pulled at his stomach like an anchor.

"I need x-rays and a head CT," the doctor said to a younger female doctor who'd joined them on the way.

"Got it," she said, taking the handoff and rolling Kate's cart through a set of sliding doors.

Jesse felt someone grab his arm. "I need you to stay with me," the doctor said, looking Jesse in the eyes.

"I can't. I need to be with her right now."

"You can't go back there. They're running some tests that I need. What I need from you is for you to tell me what happened so that I can better help her."

"It happened so fast," Jesse said.

"Why don't you sit down?" the doctor said, taking Jesse by the arm. He walked Jesse out of the emergency area and into a waiting area. "Since she's unconscious and can't tell me herself, it's important that you tell me exactly what you saw."

Jesse did his best to recount the painful events of the accident. The doctor listened, nodding now and then to let Jesse know he understood. "My name is Dr. Tilden. I'm going to check on Kate and see how the tests are going. I'll be back to update you when I have some information for you."

Dr. Tilden left Jesse alone in the waiting room. He stared at his bloodstained hands and rubbed them together, trying to wipe it all away, but it stuck to his hands like dried red paint.

Jesse prayed for Kate to pull through. The look of horror on her face from across the street when she had seen him with Sarah brought the pang of guilt back to his stomach.

"Jesse."

Jesse looked up to see Robbie, still in his Sam's Pet Shop uniform. "How's Kate?"

Jesse stood up and looked Robbie in the eye. He tried to speak, but his eyes filled with tears and his throat tightened. "It's my fault, Robbie." He crossed his arms and squeezed as if trying to keep himself from shattering into a thousand pieces. "It's my fault."

Robbie wrapped his arms around Jesse. "It's all right, little brother. I'm here, man, and we're going to get this worked out. Why don't you sit back down."

Robbie led Jesse to a group of purple vinyl-covered chairs. Jesse leaned forward with his elbows on his legs while Robbie put his hand on the back of Jesse's neck. They sat in silence as Jesse gave in to the sadness that surrounded him.

Seconds turned to minutes and still no word from the doctors. "Can I get you something?" Robbie asked. Jesse just shook his head. "Why don't you tell me what happened to Kate?"

Jesse took a deep breath, exhaling slowly. "I asked Sarah to meet me at Millennium Park. So that we could discuss…you know."

Robbie nodded but didn't interrupt him.

"We were talking about Emma, and I started thinking about…I don't know, I guess what life would've been like if I'd been there for Emma all these years. You know, if I had shown up to the coffee shop that day. And then Sarah and I almost kissed." The lump in his throat began to grow again, making it difficult for him to breathe.

"Then what happened?" Robbie asked.

"I looked across the street and saw Kate standing there. I'll never forget the look on her face. And then she took off running down the sidewalk," Jesse said, waving his hand in a forward direction. "I yelled for her to stop, but she wouldn't. I ran after her, but I was too late. She ran right out in front of a car." He looked over at Robbie. "It didn't have time to stop. And it's my fault."

"It was an accident, Jesse. You didn't know what was going to happen. And you sure as hell didn't push her in front of that car."

Jesse shook his head. "If I wouldn't have been there, then none of this would have happened."

"You have a daughter with Sarah," Robbie said. "You were only taking care of business. There's no way you could have known what would happen."

Jesse turned around when he heard the emergency room doors slide open. Dr. Tilden walked through and headed toward them. Jesse stood up. "How is she?"

"She's stable. But she has a few broken bones in her right leg, and a concussion. They're prepping an OR now so that we can go in and fix her leg."

"Is she going to be okay?" Jesse asked.

"We need to determine the extent of the damage before we can say for sure."

Jesse's eyes panned down to the floor.

"Thank you, Doctor," Robbie said.

"We'll keep you briefed as much as possible." Dr. Tilden disappeared through the emergency room doors.

Like being stuck in a bad dream, Jesse couldn't wake from this nightmare. What if she could no longer walk? What if she was in pain for the rest of her life?

"Are you okay?" Robbie asked.

Jesse looked at Robbie, a blurred vision through the tears welling in his eyes. "What if they can't fix her leg?"

Chapter Twenty

Jesse

Jesse paced up and down the hallway, waiting for the doctor's news. The more time that passed, the worse he imagined things were going.

"You're wearing a hole in the carpet," Robbie said.

"What do you think is taking so long?"

"It's only been about an hour. I'm sure they have everything handled in there. Why don't you try to relax?"

He took a seat next to Robbie. His knee bounced up and down uncontrollably. "If things aren't okay…"

"Everything's gonna be fine." Robbie placed his hand on Jesse's knee, stopping it from bouncing. "Just relax. Kate is going to need you to stay calm."

"I know." Jesse took a deep breath and sat back in his chair. "Thanks."

"For what?"

"For being here."

"Hey, it's nothin'. Besides, you're my brother. We take care of each other." Jesse forced a smile. "That's better. Now I need to step out and call Mrs. Winter to see how Maddie's doin'. Are you gonna be all right?"

Jesse nodded. "I'm fine."

"Are you sure?"

"I'm sure."

"All right. I won't be gone long." Jesse watched as Robbie disappeared into the elevators, and the pit in his stomach grew. Robbie had the ability to drive him crazy more than anyone else, but he also had the power to make him feel better when everything went pear-shaped.

Jesse stared at the emergency room doors, willing Dr. Tilden to walk through them and deliver good news, but nothing happened. He tried watching the television that was playing a rerun of Golden Girls with subtitles. But the look on Kate's face when she had seen him with Sarah kept flashing through his mind. He closed his eyes, hoping to stop the images, but they only got worse. He saw her running and remembered how desperately he wanted her to stop. To keep her away from the street. To come back to him so that he could explain that he was sorry. Sorry for hurting her, for keeping his daughter from her, for not being the man she deserved.

The sound of the emergency room doors opening caused him to open his eyes. The doctor came out, removing his surgical mask.

Jesse met him halfway. "How is she?"

"We were able to repair her right leg," Dr. Tilden said, rubbing the top of his head. "It was broken in two spots. To stabilize the break location, we had to insert titanium plates and several screws to hold it in place. Over time, the bone should fuse and heal without any long-term ramifications." He paused as if giving Jesse time to process the information. "She's pretty banged up, though. She'll be sore for a good while. And she'll be in a cast for a few weeks. After that, she'll be fitted for a brace until the muscles in her leg begin to strengthen."

"So, she's going to be okay?" Jesse asked. He held his breath as he waited for the doctor's response.

"Like I said, she's pretty banged up right now. She'll need a lot of rest. But she should be fine," he finished.

Jesse grabbed the doctor's hand and shook it vigorously. "Thank you very much, Doctor. Thank you."

The doctor just smiled. "A nurse will be out to let you know when you can see her," he said, patting Jesse on the arm.

"All right." The doctor left and Jesse took a seat. He closed his eyes and took a deep breath. A feeling of relief filled his body. He knew that they had a long road ahead of them, but she no longer faced danger, and that alone brought him a little comfort.

"You!" shouted a man from down the hall. Jesse opened his eyes and snapped his head in the direction of the voice. He watched as Christian Ashcroft, wearing a dark gray pinstriped suit, walked toward him.

"What the hell did you do to my daughter?" Jesse shot to his feet but didn't respond. "What did you do?" he demanded again.

"She was in an accident," Jesse responded.

"I'll bet she was." Christian's eyes narrowed accusingly, and a vein pulsed on the side of his neck.

Jesse did his best to ignore Christian's obvious antipathy for him. "The doctor just informed me that she's out of surgery, but no one is allowed to see her yet. He said that she's going to be fine though."

"No thanks to you," Christian said, poking his finger into Jesse's chest. "Just so you know, I did a background check on you, Jesse Malone. I know all about your sordid past." Jesse said nothing as he stared him straight in the eyes. "I had a feeling that you were dirty. You can stay away from my daughter from now on." He turned to walk toward the emergency room doors.

"That's Kate's decision," Jesse said.

Christian turned back around slowly and then walked back over to him. "You listen here, you piece of trash in a suit. My daughter is too good for you. You and your brother are—"

"Are what?" Robbie asked, walking up behind Jesse.

Christian took a look at Robbie. "You stay out of this."

"I was. You're the one who brought me into it." Robbie took a step forward and positioned himself between them. "If you have a problem with me or my brother, I'm the guy you take it up with."

Christian aimed his focus on Robbie. "I know all about you."

"Oh, I doubt that." Robbie paused and pointed his finger at Christian. "Because if you did, you wouldn't be talking to me this way."

"Is that a threat?" Christian asked.

"Let me put it in terms that you can understand." Robbie's nostrils flared as he took a deep breath. "If you don't back up now, no amount of money in the world is going to keep me from putting your ass through that wall," he said, pointing to the wall behind him.

Christian's eyes grew wide as he took a step back. Then he drew himself up, turned, and walked out of the waiting room.

Robbie turned to Jesse. "Are you okay?"

He nodded. "I'm fine."

Robbie placed his hand on Jesse's shoulder. "Well, I don't think Christmas dinner at the Ashcrofts will ever be the same."

Jesse's eyes burned from exhaustion. He leaned back in his chair and closed them, hoping the nurse would be out soon and tell him it was time to see Kate.

***

"Are you here for Kate Ashcroft?"

Jesse woke up and rubbed his eyes. He saw a nurse standing above him. "That's me," he replied.

"You can go in and see her now," the nurse said.

Jesse stood up a bit too quickly and had to place a hand on Robbie's shoulder to steady himself. "Which room?"

"She's in a recovery room." The nurse pointed down a hall. "You head down the hall, take a left, and she's in room 312."

"Okay." Jesse stood up. "How's she doing?"

"Right now she's sleeping. She's been through a lot."

"Thank you."

"If she needs anything, just ask for me. My name's Renea."

"Thank you," he repeated.

"You're welcome." The nurse walked down the hall and disappeared into one of the rooms.

"I'm going to go see how she's doing. You can go home if you want. You probably need to get some sleep."

"No," Robbie objected. Then he yawned and stretched. "I'm fine right here. Besides, Ricky likes having a break from me." He checked his watched. "And Maddie'll be asleep by now."

"All right, I'll be back."

"Good luck."

"Thank you."

Robbie just nodded and picked up a magazine.

Jesse walked down the hall. Each step felt heavier than the last. When he reached room 312, he paused. Only a soft ray of light shone through the doorway. He gathered what little courage he had left and walked inside. The dark room was lit only by the small light above her bed. White bandages covered part of her face. The exposed parts of her face puffed out like she'd had an allergic reaction to something.

Jesse took a seat next to her bed, careful not to wake her. He reached over and grabbed her hand. He noticed her engagement ring. Jesse had spent months looking for the perfect ring, but he couldn't decide which one she would love the most. So, he had scheduled a meeting with the store owner and explained the situation. He agreed to allow Jesse to take three rings home. Jesse had planned an elaborate dinner for her, and at the end of the meal, he had presented her with three large cupcakes, each with a sign sticking out with one word. PLEASE. MARRY. ME. And resting on each sign was one of the rings. He remembered the surprised look on her face. And for the first time since he'd known her, she was speechless. He set the cupcakes in front of her on the table and then got down on one knee. *Kate, I searched for the perfect ring for you, but there are none in this world that match your perfection. If one of these rings seems a worthy reflection of our love, I would be honored if you would accept it as a token of my love and commitment to you and agree to be my wife. I promise to take care of you and show you every day how exceptional you are.*

Kate had picked up one of the chocolate iced cupcakes and removed the princess-cut diamond ring. *It is absolutely beautiful*, she had gushed, throwing her arms around him as if she'd never let go.

One of the machines next to Kate let out a series of beeps, bringing Jesse back to the hospital room, his fiancée's hand in his. He tried to bite back the tears, but the sadness won. He pressed his lips to her hand. "I'm so sorry, Kate."

Chapter Twenty-one

Jesse

Jesse stared at the tubes running from Kate's forearm and leading toward an IV, which stood next to a machine monitoring her heart. He watched the line rise and fall with her heartbeat, letting himself get lost in the quiet rhythm of her breathing.

A few minutes passed before she opened her eyes. He smiled and said, "Hey, baby. I'm right here." She looked around the room and then at Jesse. She didn't smile or frown. She simply blinked a few times and then fell back to sleep.

"Get some sleep. I'm not going anywhere."

Jesse sat by her side for the next few hours. Christian and Kate's mother, Laura, came in to visit. Jesse stood up and took a seat in the back of the room, making room for them. Laura sat in the chair where Jesse had been sitting and cried over Kate's sleeping body. She ran her hand through Kate's hair in a practiced motion, as if she'd done that a thousand times before. Christian stood on the other side of the bed. He held Kate's hand and shot Jesse an occasional look of disgust. Jesse just looked away. He thought more than once about leaving to remove the tension from the room, but he couldn't bring himself to leave Kate's side.

They stayed for a few hours before heading to the cafeteria for coffee. Jesse stood and Laura walked over to him. "Please take care of my baby," she said as she wrapped her arms around him.

"I will," he said, then whispered, "I'm so sorry."

When they separated, she locked eyes with Jesse and said, "I know, Jesse." Of Kate's entire family, it was her mother who had been the one who'd welcomed him in and treated him like family. He wished he had gotten to know her better through the years they'd been together, but the opportunity never presented itself. He saw the genuine pain in her eyes, and he hated himself for hurting both Kate and her mother.

After they left the room, Jesse walked back over to Kate and sat next her. He took her hand and rubbed her arm. Her eyes opened again, and with a faint and raspy voice she said, "Jesse?"

"Yes, it's me, baby. How are you feeling?"

Her head moved from side to side as her eyes continued to open and shut as if she was trying to fight sleep. Then she tried to raise her head, but stopped, wincing in pain. Jesse straightened her pillows to make her a little more comfortable. She blinked a few times and looked around. "My head hurts," she said.

"You're in a hospital, sweetheart."

She looked around again and then lifted her arm to get a better look at the IV lines. "How did I get here?"

"You were in an accident, baby," he replied. "Is there something I can get you?"

She licked her lips and made a face as if she'd tasted something awful. "I'm thirsty."

"Here," Jesse said, holding up a cup of water. "The nurse said it was okay for you to have this, but you have to take small sips." Jesse brought the cup to her lips and carefully lifted her head so that she could drink.

"Thank you," she said. "What happened?"

"You were hit by a car."

She reached up and felt the bandages on her head. Jesse could see a worried look forming on her face. "You're going to be okay. The doctor had to fix your right leg. And the rest are just scratches that will heal quickly." Kate looked down at her leg, but it was covered in a blanket.

"How did this happen?" she asked.

Jesse hesitated, not sure how to tell her. "Are you sure you want to hear this now?" She nodded. "Do you remember Millennium Park?"

She looked up at the ceiling as if searching for the answer there. "I'm not sure. I remember that I was giving a product demonstration when someone called and said that you wanted to meet me at the park. I think."

"Who called you?"

"I can't remember."

"Was it a man or a woman?"

Her eyes narrowed as she searched her memory bank. She raised a hand to her head. "My head hurts so bad."

Jesse placed his hand on her shoulder. "That's okay, baby. Don't worry about it now."

"I do remember that it was a beautiful day. I thought you wanted to take a walk at..."

Jesse could tell by the look in her eyes that she'd registered something, but he had no idea what it was. His stomach flipped and he held his breath.

She looked at Jesse with the same eyes that he'd seen when she found him with Sarah, and he knew that she knew. "You should lie back down," he said.

"Wait," she said. "I do remember seeing you." Her raspy voice grew louder. "You were with the woman from the flower shop."

Jesse dropped his head in response. "Sarah," he said.

"That's right! You two were sitting on a bench and..." She paused. Her eyes grew large as tears welled.

"Nothing happened."

"It looked like more than nothing to me."

"I stopped it before it started."

She set her head back onto the pillow. "There shouldn't have been anything to stop."

Jesse held her hand. "I'm so sorry, Kate."

"Who is she? Who is she really?"

He leaned forward and rubbed her arm. "She was someone I met when I was just a little kid. Back then, I didn't have many friends. My life was..." He paused. "Let's just say that it was difficult."

"What does that mean?" she asked, lifting her head and looking into his eyes.

"When we met and you asked about my parents, I told you that they had passed away. I told you that it was an accident and that I didn't like talking about it." As much as he hated reliving this story, he knew that Kate deserved the truth. "My dad was a drunk. A mean one. One day my mom waited until he was on the road. He was a trucker. She grabbed my brother and me and we left town. Mom was trying to keep us safe—as far away from him as we

127

could get. We moved around a lot during that time, so he couldn't find us. That's how we ended up in New Haven and when I met Sarah."

Jesse stared at the darkness through the window. Short clips of the memory of his darkest day played in his head. The blood covering his mother's face. The way his dad had held her lifeless body in the air like a doll before dropping her straight to the floor. "I came home one day and found his pickup in the driveway. He had found us." A lump formed in his throat making it difficult to speak. "He had already beaten my mother to death when I walked in. Robbie had been knocked to the ground, so I had to do something. I had to protect my brother and myself. So I picked up a knife and…"

Jesse saw the shock on Kate's face. "I had no idea."

"It's not something I like to talk about."

"I can see why."

"My brother and I were placed in the care of my Uncle August and Aunt Sherry, which is how we ended up in Chicago. I never had the chance to tell Sarah goodbye. She had been the one person who brought peace into my life, and suddenly she was gone. But, I was in a new place, a new school with new friends, and I loved having a fresh start. I missed Sarah terribly, but she was a part of that past, too, so I had to let her go."

"Then you and your uncle opened the pet shop?"

"That's right. When he retired, he thought it would be something fun for us share, help us learn responsibility and all," he replied. "When Sarah walked into the pet shop six years ago, it had been ten years since I'd last seen her.

Apparently she'd moved to Chicago with her dad after her mom had left them."

Kate didn't speak. She just listened as Jesse continued telling his story. "Well, we started hanging out, but just as friends. She was engaged to someone at the time." He paused again and searched for the right words to say. "But the more we hung out, the more we started to develop feelings for each other."

"I can see how that could happen," Kate replied. "Especially since she was the one who offered a friendship to you when you were going through all of that stuff as a kid."

Jesse nodded and continued his story. "Things had already started to get weird between us, but then her dad died, and things really got weird. We ended up spending a night together and…" Kate turned to the ceiling and closed her eyes. Jesse wished he could stop. Stop hurting her more than she already hurt, but he knew that if he stopped now, he'd never work up the nerve to tell her everything. "We never meant for anything to happen. It just did," he said.

"Then what happened?" Kate asked with disdain in her voice.

"I left," Jesse said. "That's when I went back to college and to New York, leaving everything else behind. And I hadn't heard from or seen her since the night we spent together."

"Until you and I walked into the flower shop a few weeks ago?" Kate asked.

Jesse nodded.

"Why didn't you tell me the truth?" she asked. "As the woman who was planning to marry you, don't you think I deserved the truth?"

"I don't know why I didn't tell you," Jesse responded. "I guess I thought it was because it was so long ago."

"Then why now?" Kate asked as she looked Jesse in the eyes. "Why did you go to the park with her? Why were you guys sitting on the bench together? And why did you..."

Jesse looked down. The time had arrived to tell her everything. The lump in his throat grew, as if it somehow knew what it would mean to tell Kate everything. He ran a hand through his hair and took a deep breath. "Because I have a daughter."

"What?!" Kate winced and touched the side of her head.

"Are you okay? Can I get you anything?"

She shook her head. "I'm fine. Keep going."

"Sarah and I have a daughter together," he replied.

"You have a daughter and you never told me?" Her voice cracked, revealing the last of the seams that had been keeping her together.

"I found out just a few weeks ago. I stopped by the flower shop and there she was." He remembered her long brown hair and blue eyes. A mini version of his mother. "I had a hard time believing it myself. I decided to meet with Sarah to talk about what I...what we were going to do."

Kate turned her head toward the window on the opposite wall. "It's like I don't even know who you are."

"Yes, you do," Jesse said. "I'm the same man you fell in love with. The same man who's here for you now."

"It's like you have two lives. The one you've been living with me and the one you chose to keep hidden from me," she said. "Even when you found out you had a child, your initial reaction was to hide it from me."

"I'm sorry." Desperation grew along with the lump in his throat. "I'll tell you everything. Anything you want to know."

She turned back toward Jesse. Her eyes were full of tears now. "Do you love me?"

Jesse leaned forward and grabbed her hand. "Of course I do."

"Do you love her?"

Jesse paused. A simple, short, yet definite pause that said it all. "She was the first and only girl I had ever loved, until I met you."

The tears rolled down her cheeks, and Jesse hated himself for each one of them. "I can't do this."

"Do what?" he asked.

"I can't get married. Not to you, not now."

"Because I have a daughter? That doesn't change anything between us," he said.

"You're right, that doesn't change anything. You never told me about your childhood, about your parents, about Sarah. And now you have a daughter that you didn't know about. Jesse Malone, I don't know who you are anymore." She wiped tears from her cheeks and removed the engagement ring from her finger.

Jesse could no longer hold back his own tears. "Don't do this, Kate," he said, shaking his head. "I love you."

"I love you, Jesse." She took his hand and turned it palm up. "But I can't marry you. Not now."

Jesse looked at the diamond sitting in the palm of his hand. A tear fell from his cheek and shattered onto the ring, breaking his heart into a million pieces.

Chapter Twenty-two

Sarah

Sarah watched as Emma walked hand-in-hand with her mom up the tiny hill. The wind lifted strands of her brown hair like tiny kites. It had been about six years now since Sarah's mother had come back in her life, and things still felt a little...weird. She loved her mother, there was no denying that, and had somehow found it in her heart to truly forgive her for abandoning her when she was just a teenager. But their adult relationship had become more like that of a friendship than one of mother and daughter. The scars her mother had left must have been too tough for their connection to grow deeper. But not for Emma. She only knew life with Grandma Evelyn in it. And she loved her like she was the best grandma in the whole world. And in many ways, she was. A part of Sarah often wondered if she subconsciously held that against her mother.

"Can we get ice cream after this?"

Evelyn looked back at Sarah. "It's up to your mom."

"Can we, Mom?"

"Why not?"

A smile formed on Emma's face, revealing her dimples.

"Why don't you take these and run ahead?" Sarah handed her a gorgeous bouquet of flowers. An arrangement she only did on special occasions. "I want to talk to Grandma."

"Why can't I listen?" Emma pouted.

Sarah knelt down to Emma's level. "Sweetie, it's boring grownup talk. You wouldn't like it anyway."

"But I understand grownup talk. I've been five for a long time now."

"Yes, you have. And you're getting so big, too. But the stuff we're going to talk about is boring. You don't want to hear that stuff, do you?"

She wrinkled her nose and shook her head.

"Why don't you run ahead. You remember the way, right?"

Emma nodded and pointed. "That way."

"That's right. You are getting to be so big." Sarah gave her a hug and stood up.

They watched as Emma took off running. Her hair flew behind her like a superhero's cape.

"She's definitely getting big," Sarah's mother said.

"I know. And I swear I feel more and more like I don't know what I'm doing the older she gets."

"That's normal."

"Is it? Because I feel like I've made a complete mess of everything."

A cool breeze came in, blowing her mom's long blonde hair into her face. "That's normal, too."

Her words did little to soothe Sarah. She felt a pang of guilt for what had happened to Kate. She knew she had to make things right again. With Kate, with Jesse, and with Emma. "I don't know what to do."

"First of all, you have to stop being so hard on yourself." She looked toward Emma who was nearly halfway to their destination. "She's a perfectly healthy and happy little girl. And you did that. Despite everything that you've been through over the past few years with Kevin and now with this divorce, you've managed to still provide your little girl with a good and happy life. That's all any parent can hope to do. More than I was able to do."

She placed a hand on her mom's arm. "Mom, don't."

She shook her head. "It's okay. I know how badly I messed up with you. I missed out on some of the most critical years of your childhood. Your father did a wonderful job raising you. Look at Emma. She's proof of the woman you've turned out to be. Your father was the most wonderful man I have ever known."

Sarah turned away and bit back tears. "He was pretty great."

"So, what are you going to do about Jesse?"

"I don't know what to do. I called the hospital to see how Kate was doing, but they wouldn't tell me. So, I asked Rachael to have her mom, who's a nurse there, take a peek for me. And I guess she's doing much better."

"Well, that's good." Evelyn looked at Emma who had stopped and stared at the flowers in her hand. "You have to stop beating yourself up over what happened. It was an accident."

"I know. But if I hadn't almost kissed Jesse, none of this would have happened to begin with."

"What you should be thinking about is why you and Jesse almost kissed."

She looked at her mom, an almost mirror image of herself, but that's where the similarity ended. On the inside, she was much more like her father. "It was a mistake.

Nothing more. Two people caught up in a sentimental moment, remembering who they used to be and forgetting who they are now."

"But maybe it's because who you used to be is better than who you are now. Have you thought of that?"

"No, I guess I've been too busy thinking about the woman whose life was almost lost."

Her mom started walking toward Emma and Sarah followed. "Sarah, it wasn't your fault. You can keep beating yourself up if you want, but it will never be your fault." She pointed to Emma. "But that little girl does have a dad out there. And I of all people know how wrong it is to keep her from him."

Sarah let out a deep breath. "I just don't want anyone else getting hurt. And I don't know how Em's going to handle it."

"Well, I've never met the man, but from what you've told me over the past six years, Jesse seems like he'd be a fine father."

"It's not that simple. It's not like he's signed up for this. He didn't even know she existed until recently."

Evelyn shot Sarah a stern look. "Don't get me started on that."

"Do you see what I mean? I've messed everything up."

Evelyn threw up her hands. "So, maybe you have. However, it's in the past now. What matters is what you do now. For you. And for this precious little girl." She placed a hand on Emma's head as they reached her and stroked her hair.

"Who's precious?" Emma asked.

"You are," Sarah replied.

"Are you guys still talking grownup stuff?"

Sarah shook her head. "No. We're all done. Do you want to do the honors?"

Emma nodded and smiled. Then she turned toward the stone and placed the flowers on top of it. "Happy Birthday, Grandpa."

Evelyn walked over and brushed some leaves from the stone, revealing the name STANLEY RAMSEY. She kissed her fingers and then touched the stone. "I miss you so much."

Sarah stood behind Emma and put her hands on her shoulders so that she wouldn't see her crying.

"Mommy?"

"Yes, baby?"

"Do you think Grandpa would've liked me?"

"Sweetie, he would have loved you."

"Can you tell me the story again about how you guys sat under the willow tree and fished?"

Evelyn placed a hand on Sarah's shoulder, and with her other hand, she wiped tears from her cheeks. Sarah touched her mother's hand and then crouched down beside Emma. "Once upon a time…"

Emma smiled. "It's like a fairy tale."

"That's right, baby. It was Mommy's fairy tale."

Chapter Twenty-three

Sarah

A few days had passed since the day Sarah had met Jesse at the park. He still hadn't contacted her, but she didn't hold that against him. He'd been through a lot in a short amount of time. More than anyone deserved. And she wasn't about to make things worse by contacting him. Instead, she had something else in mind.

The elevator sounded off a subtle beep with each passing floor. And with each beep, her stomach coiled and twisted. Then it came to a stop. She closed her eyes and took a deep breath and waited for the doors to slide open. She took a step into the hall, but her feet wouldn't take another step. She watched as nurses and doctors passed by her, going about their busy lives, completely unaware of the torment living within her.

"Can I help you?"

Sarah turned to a pleasant-looking nurse with dark hair in a ponytail and pink scrubs.

"I'm not sure. I'm looking for someone."

"A patient?"

Sarah nodded. "I think so."

The nurse stared at her as if expecting more, but Sarah said nothing. "Do you know the patient's name?"

"Ashcroft. Kate Ashcroft."

"She's down that hall and to the left. Room 517."

Sarah stared down the hall and nodded. "Okay, thank you."

"No problem," said the nurse. Then she took off, disappearing into one of the rooms.

Sarah went to room 517 and saw Kate sitting up in her bed, watching television. Some sort of a cast enclosed her right leg and various bandages covered her right hand and part of her face. A shroud of guilt covered Sarah, like a suffocating blanket. "Kate?"

Kate turned and saw Sarah. Her eyes held a look of disdain, telling Sarah how unwelcome she was. "I'm sorry. I can go." Sarah turned around.

"No!" Kate snapped.

Sarah froze and slowly turned around.

"Why don't you come in? I would like to talk to you."

Sarah took a few steps inside and then stopped.

Kate motioned to the chair next to her bed. "Please, take a seat."

"Thank you."

Kate lifted her remote and turned off the television. "I'm glad you came here."

"You are?" For a moment Sarah wondered what kind of pain meds they had her on.

"Yes. I wanted to ask you if you're in love with Jesse."

Taken aback, Sarah shook her head. "He's just someone I used to care about a long time ago."

"That's not what I saw."

Sarah shifted in her seat. "That's why I came here. I wanted to tell you that nothing happened between Jesse and me."

Kate crossed her arms. "If it was nothing, then what would you call what I saw?"

"It was a mistake. I don't know what Jesse's told you, but things are somewhat complicated between us. We have…"

"A daughter," Kate supplied.

"That's right," Sarah replied.

"So, does that give you the right to get between Jesse and me?"

"No," she said, shaking her head. "And that's why I came here. I want to apologize for everything. I know that there's nothing I can do to fix this," Sarah said, motioning to Kate's leg. "There's no way for me to explain how sorry I am for the pain I've caused you." She looked down at the purse in her lap. Her fingers picked at the leather straps. "I just wanted my daughter to know her father."

"I understand that."

Sarah looked up at Kate. Her arms were uncrossed and her face had softened. "If I could go back and change things, I would."

"It's okay. What's done is done."

Sarah stood up. "I'd completely understand if you didn't want me to handle your wedding flowers. But they would be free of charge, of course. It's the least I can do."

"That won't be necessary," Kate said. "The wedding has been cancelled."

"Why? Because of me?"

"No, although that didn't help matters. It's more than that."

Sarah tucked a strand of hair behind her ear. "I'm sorry to hear that."

Kate didn't respond, and Sarah took that as her cue to leave. She turned and headed toward the door. Before walking out of the room, she turned back to Kate. "I know it's none of my business, but I think it's a mistake to let him go. He's a good guy, with a big heart. And he loves you so much."

"How do you know? You don't know anything about me."

"I don't have to know you to know how Jesse feels about you."

"Why do you say that?"

"Because Jesse Malone doesn't just give his heart out to anyone."

Kate glanced down at her left hand. "It's too late."

Sarah noted the lack of a ring on Kate's ring finger. "Don't make the same mistake that I made," Sarah said. "He's worth fighting for."

Chapter Twenty-four

Robbie

Not a day went by that Madison didn't do something that reminded Robbie of her mother. The way she smiled, the way she laughed, even now when she reached up for Robbie's hand as they walked down the sidewalk, she reminded him of Felicia. It was what she had done every time they took their walks when she was pregnant with Maddie. They had spent hours walking down the sidewalks of Chicago, talking about the future, about the precious gift growing inside her belly. They wondered whose eyes she would have, or whose nose she'd have. Robbie had hoped she'd take more after Felicia than himself. And when it came to personality, well, he had been a bit of a hard case until Felicia walked into his life. She had saved him, pulled him from the life of crime he had so often gravitated toward, and once again, Maddie reminded him of her mother.

"Are we almost there?" she asked.

He looked down and smiled. With one hand in his and her stuffed bunny in the other, she melted his heart with the ease of warm butter on hot bread. "Almost, baby girl."

"Good, because Bunny's getting tired of all of this walking."

They walked another block before they arrived at Jesse's office. His boutique architect firm resided in an old historic building that he shared with accountants and attorneys. Robbie opened the door for her. "After you."

"Thank you, sir." She took one look at Nina and her face lit up like a Christmas tree.

"Hey there, Madison. I didn't know you guys were stopping by today."

"That's because it's a surprise. We're here to cheer up Uncle Jesse."

Nina looked at Robbie, and he shrugged. "I'm sorry, she's not very subtle. We're gonna have to work on that."

"No, I think it's a great idea. He definitely could use some cheering up, and I'll bet you're the one who can do it, too." She pointed down the hall. "Head on back. He's going to be so happy to see you."

"Thank you."

"No problem. I'm glad you're here. He's been kind of worrying me lately. The past few weeks have been so rough on him."

"I'll bet," Robbie agreed. "Ponyboy's definitely had it rough."

They walked down the hall and knocked on the frosted glass door that led to his office.

"Come in."

Madison opened the door slowly and then ran inside. "Uncle Jesse!" She ran around his desk and straight into his arms.

"Peanut, it's so good to see you."

She kept her tiny arms wrapped around his neck and looked him in the eyes as if examining him. "You don't look sad. Just tired."

Jesse chuckled. "Someone told you that I was sad, huh?"

She smiled, nodded, and then whispered, "It's a secret."

"Well, I'm not sad anymore. I'm just so glad to see you."

"And Bunny?" She held up her favorite stuffed animal.

"And Bunny, too."

"Sorry for dropping by like this. We just got back from the park, and she had asked about you. So, I thought it would be better to just stop by so she could see you," Robbie explained.

"I'm glad you did."

"Excuse me," Nina said, poking her head through the doorway. "But I was about to go get some ice cream. I don't suppose anyone would want to go with me."

"I would!" Madison turned to Jesse. "Do you want ice cream, too?"

"No, Peanut. I'm pretty busy right now. Maybe next time."

She dropped down from Jesse's lap and walked up to Robbie. "Is it okay if I get some ice cream with Nina?"

"Okay, but make sure you listen to her and do as she says."

"I will."

They walked out of the office, leaving Robbie and Jesse alone. Robbie took a seat in front of his desk. "So, how have things been? I haven't heard you from since the... you know."

"I've been busy. The bid came back and we got the Drake project."

"Are you serious?"

Jesse nodded and flashed a forced smile.

"Wow, that is awesome, man. You should be celebrating right now."

"I haven't really been in the mood lately."

"How's Kate?"

Jesse reached into his pocket, pulled out a diamond ring, and set it on the desk. "Does that answer your question?"

Robbie shook his head. "Man, I am so sorry. I had no idea."

Jesse shrugged. "I haven't heard from her since the day of the accident. I've tried calling her parents to see how she's doing, but like her, they refuse to answer my calls."

"That really sucks, man. I know how much she means to you."

"Yeah, well, I messed that up pretty good."

"You need to stop beating yourself up, man. Things happen and there's nothing you can do about it. It's just a bum deal is all."

Jesse stared at the ring as if lost in deep thought.

"There is something else I came here to talk to you about." Jesse gave his attention back to Robbie. "With everything going on, I didn't have a chance to tell you this, but I stopped by Sarah's flower shop."

"I know. Sarah told me."

"I wanted to apologize for throwing out the letter and for...well, you know. Anyway, I also stopped by to see my niece. Who is absolutely adorable, by the way. She and

Maddie totally hit it off. It was like they had known each other their whole lives. That Emma seems like a clever little girl." Robbie rubbed his chin. "Must be a Malone thing."

"Don't flatter yourself."

"Like I said, I was there to apologize, but I ran into that pompous jerk, Kevin. He was walking out as I was walking in and he flashed that stupid smile."

"I bet that was awkward."

"At first I didn't know it was him. I just thought he looked familiar. It wasn't until I saw the broken vases on the floor and was talking to Sarah that I remembered who he was."

"Broken vases?"

"Yeah, and Sarah looked real frazzled if you know what I mean."

Jesse's eyes narrowed. "What are you trying to say?"

"I think he's gettin' rough with her. The way she avoided eye contact, blamed the broken vases on being 'clumsy,' and she just seemed…upset about something. That's when I remembered that stupid smile. I'm tellin' you, man, I think this dude's trouble."

Jesse took a deep breath and leaned back into his seat. "Are you sure about his?"

Robbie had a sense about things like this. After years of watching their mother take abuse from their father, he had become sort of a divining rod to this kind of stuff. "You know I'm sure. What are you gonna do?"

"What can I do?"

"I don't know, man. But that's your daughter over there. You've got to do something."

Jesse didn't respond.

"You do realize that you have a daughter, right?"

"What the hell is that supposed to mean?"

"You know what it means, man. You have a little girl, and you haven't moved an inch to get to know her. It's not right."

"Oh really, and what is right? Walking up to Emma and saying, 'Hey there, you know that guy with the slicked back hair who you've always known as your dad? Well, he's not. I'm your real dad.' I'm sure that would go over real well."

"I can't believe this."

Jesse threw up his arms. "Believe what? That I don't know what to do? Well, I don't!"

"Be a father. It's that simple. Listen, I know you've been dealt a crappy hand, and I know that it's not your first, but you have a little girl who needs you right now. So, step up and be a dad."

"Yeah, well maybe I would have stood half a chance if I hadn't bailed you out of trouble."

"What's that supposed to mean?"

"Forget I said anything." Jesse placed his elbows on his desk and picked up a blueprint.

"What do you mean, you would have stood half a chance if you hadn't bailed me out?"

"You really want to get into this?"

Robbie leaned forward, his blood pressure rising like steam in a teakettle. "Humor me."

"You remember that day I stood Sarah up?"

Robbie nodded. "What does that have to do with this?"

Jesse sat forward and looked Robbie in the eyes. "I did it for you."

Chapter Twenty-five

Jesse

For six years, Jesse had kept secret the fact that he had traded a life with Sarah for Robbie's freedom. Until now. And he immediately wished he could take it back. Robbie reacted the way he expected. Explosively.

Jesse bent over and picked up the items that had fallen from his desk when Robbie slammed his fist onto it, just before storming out of his office. Jesse had tried to apologize, but when that didn't work, he explained that if given a chance to change things, he wouldn't. He owed Robbie.

When the world thought that Robbie had killed their father—the monster—he went ahead and took the heat for it. He shielded Jesse from the years of torture and torment that followed, and, for the most part, he ignored it when people pointed and jeered at the "murdering son." But, eventually he realized he had only one defense that would help get him through life: his fists. He began taking on anyone who gave him and Jesse trouble, and he started chasing a life of crime, which ultimately landed him in jail. Sure he was the one who they found breaking and entering, but what his criminal report didn't reflect was the crappy hand life had dealt him. Through it all, Jesse had kept silent about the truth. But the day had come for him to do right by Robbie.

By then, Robbie had Felicia and a baby on the way; he couldn't just let his brother rot in prison now. Not after all he'd been through. So, he made a deal with the devil. And Kevin had lived up to his end of the bargain. One week after Jesse watched Sarah accept Kevin's ring, Kevin arranged for Robbie to be released from prison, giving him a second chance at making things right for Felicia and their baby.

Jesse heard his door open behind him. "Listen, man. I said I was sorry. Can't you see why I did it?"

"Did what?"

Jesse looked over his shoulder and saw a set of crutches and a large pink cast. "Kate?"

"Hey, Jesse."

He stood up and helped her to the chair across from his desk. "What are you doing here? I mean, I'm glad that you're here, but I'm not sure why you are. Not that you're not welcome, because you are. I was just wondering why you're…"

She let out a soft laugh. "It's okay. I know what you mean."

"How are you feeling? I tried calling but…"

"I know." She paused with a smile so perfect all he could think about was how he missed feeling the energy of her lips pressed against his. "I'm fine." She set her crutches on the floor beside her and then placed a hand on her leg. "My leg is doing much better now."

"That's great. Have you been staying with your parents?"

Kate nodded. "After I left the hospital, I had some things that I needed to think about."

The tie around Jesse's neck felt like it was choking him, like a snake drawing tighter and tighter. He grabbed the knot and loosened it. "I understand."

"Relax, Jesse. I didn't come here to fight."

Jesse just smiled.

"So, who did you think you were you talking to when I walked in?"

Jesse sat at the end of his desk and folded his hands together. "Yeah. Sorry about that. I thought you were Robbie. He was here earlier and we had an argument. Then he stormed out before I could...well, he's gone now."

Kate pointed to his messy desk. "Must've been a pretty serious argument."

"Robbie can be quite unreasonable sometimes."

"Well, that makes two of us then."

"What do you mean?"

She looked at her pink cast. A pang of guilt filled his stomach as he looked at it. "I, too, can be unreasonable sometimes."

"I disagree. I think you are the definition of reasonable."

She looked up at Jesse and a faint smile flashed across her face. "I shouldn't have reacted the way I did. I should have tried to put myself in—"

"You had every right to react the way you did, Kate. I totally understand."

"Let me finish, and I think you'll understand."

Jesse nodded.

"Do you remember when we first started dating? Before you ever moved to New York for school?"

Jesse had no idea how this could have anything to do with how he hurt her now, but he nodded.

"I fell in love with you back then, but you were closed off from love—wanted nothing to do with such a commitment. I stayed though, because I thought you'd come around. That you would wake up and someday see what we had together. But you never did." And just when Jesse thought he couldn't feel worse, he did. Kate continued. "When you moved to New York, I was crushed. I couldn't get you out of my mind."

"Is that why you decided to open a salon in New York?"

"No. That was a good business opportunity. But since I knew you were in New York, well, I couldn't resist looking you up and inviting you to dinner."

"Naturally." Jesse ran a hand down his tie, feigning confidence.

"As I was saying, when you moved to New York, I really missed you. And for the first time in my life, I felt what it was like to lose someone you care about." She paused and Jesse could see tears welling in her eyes, breaking his heart. "When I saw you at the park that day with...her," she grabbed a tissue from her purse and dabbed her eyes, "I thought to myself, I'm going to lose him again. And I freaked out."

Jesse got up from his desk and walked over to Kate, kneeling beside her chair. "Kate, I am so sorry. I'm sorry you felt like you lost me when I moved to New York, and I'm sorry for the pain I caused through all of this. I never ever meant to hurt you."

"I know, Jesse. You're a good guy and you have a big heart. I've been replaying everything you told me ever since the last time I saw you, and, if I'd just put myself in your shoes, I'd have realized how difficult and confusing things were for you. I should have been more reasonable."

A brief light of hope warmed his heart. "Does this mean that you forgive me?"

She nodded. "I'm sorry I can't get down on one knee, but Jesse Malone, will you marry me?"

A lump formed in the back of Jesse's throat. He stood up and grabbed the engagement ring from atop his desk and got down on one knee. Kate held out her hand with tears running down her cheeks, and Jesse slid the ring onto her finger.

Chapter Twenty-six

Sarah

Rachael picked up a scrappy looking cat from the shelf of overflowing stuffed animals and held it up. "What about this?"

Sarah shot her an are-you-serious look. "She likes dogs. And if she did like cats, she probably wouldn't want one that looked that mean."

Rachael took another look at its face. "I don't know, it's kind of cute. In a…" she tried pulling back its ears and smoothing the fur from its face. "Nope, it's just plain scary." And then she tossed it back on the shelf. "You see, this is why you're the mom and I'm like the crazy aunt who's not really related to you guys."

Sarah often thought of Rachael as a sister, but never gave much thought about her being like an aunt to Emma. But she had to agree with Rachael, she was glad that she was Emma's mom. "One of these days you might change your mind about being a mom. Kids have a way of stealing your heart."

"I can see that with Emma. I don't know how she does it, but whenever I look into those gorgeous blue eyes, I feel like she can make me do just about anything." Sarah chuckled. "So, are you going to tell me what's been going on with you? You haven't mentioned Jesse since the day of…well, since the day you saw him at the park."

Sarah placed both hands on the cart and took a few steps down the aisle with Rachael next to her. "I went to see Kate."

"You did!?"

Sarah nodded. "I had to apologize."

"And what did she say?"

"That things were over between her and Jesse."

Rachael placed her hand on the side of the cart, stopping it from moving forward. "Do you realize what this means?"

"That you are a horrible person for thinking what you're thinking right now."

"Oh, come on. It's perfect."

"What's perfect? That someone was hurt badly, and nearly killed, over something I had done."

"Whatever. You didn't do anything. You guys didn't even kiss."

"It doesn't matter. When she saw the two of us together, she…" Sarah paused, remembering the horrible scene, wishing that she could erase it from her mind.

Rachael placed her hands on Sarah's shoulder. "Listen, I'm not saying that you and Jesse should get married this weekend. Although I could put something together pretty quickly for you. But can't you at least think about what life would be like with you and Jesse and Emma?"

"You think I haven't thought about that? Emma's my little girl. Nothing means more to me than she does, and I know how incredible it would be if she had Jesse around every day of her life. But at what cost? I can't do that to

Kate. I can't do that to Jesse. I won't destroy something good just to get what I want."

Rachael let go and they started walking down the aisle. "So, let me guess," she paused to look back at Sarah. "You told her that letting go of Jesse was a mistake."

Sarah nodded. "I had to."

"You can't tell me that there isn't a small part of you that doesn't still love Jesse. I see the way you light up every time we talk about him."

"Jesse and I shared something that's rare. All that time spent beneath the willow tree. I know we were just kids, but he really took care of me when I needed him the most. And he did that given everything else he had going on in his life. Then he was there for me when my dad died. He's different." She looked down and shook her head. "He's…Jesse."

"Oh my gosh! You are totally in love with that man. I don't know why you aren't with him right now."

"A part of me will always love him. And that's why I told Kate what I did. I did it for Jesse, too."

"You love him, so you made it possible for him to be with another woman?" Rachael's sarcastic tone rang loud and clear.

Sarah nodded. "I had to. It was the right thing to do. If there's a chance for them to be happy together, I can't stand in the way of that."

Rachael shook her head. "But he's so…"

"Great," Sarah said, finishing Rachael's sentence. "Trust me, I know."

"I was going to say hot, but great works, too."

"You really are terrible, Rach."

"Speaking of terrible, what's going on with Kevin? Is he still being his usual creepy self?"

Sarah picked up a stuffed giraffe and studied its face. "I don't know what to do about him. Ever since he started having problems at work, he's been acting so strange. I know we had our issues in the past, but I've never seen him like this before."

"You know what you have to do, Sarah."

She turned to Rachael and saw concern in her face. "It's not that simple. You know who his father is. And despite his legal problems right now, he still has friends who are lawyers and police officers."

"He's getting worse." She walked over to Sarah. "Do you think I don't notice the worried expression on your face whenever you're looking out the window?"

"It's complicated. Even though he isn't Emma's biological father, he's the only father she knows."

"And that gives him the right to stalk you?"

"No," Sarah let out a sigh. "I know. I know. I'm just scared."

"I know you are. But that's why you have me. I might be the only one he's afraid of."

Sarah let out another chuckle. "I think you're right there."

Rachael wrapped her arm around Sarah's shoulder and gave her an encouraging squeeze. "You have to stand up to him, Sarah. You can do this."

"I know." Sarah spotted an adorable stuffed dog on the bottom shelf amongst a row of turtles. "How about that one?"

Rachael followed her line of sight and picked it up, giving it a huge hug. "Aw, this one reminds me of my Mutt."

"Rach, you are so gross."

Chapter Twenty-seven

Jesse

With less than a week before his wedding, Jesse started to settle back into a hectic, yet comfortable, routine. On most mornings, Jesse would have a cab drop him off a few blocks from his office, allowing him time to clear his head and take in the architectural wonders that the city of Chicago had to offer. The walk inspired him, igniting a sense of passion that fueled him for the day. With the Drake project underway, he needed the inspiration even more. But today was too hot for the walk, so he had the cab drop him at the entrance.

As usual, Nina had beaten him to work. He saw a stack of paperwork from the contractors sitting on her desk. She knew just as well as he did that they needed to wrap up some of their other projects before they got started on the Drake renovations. She held up a cup of coffee as he walked by. He couldn't have been more thrilled when she had agreed to stay on for another semester. He had grown to depend on her in ways he never thought he would. And he definitely didn't want to have to replace her now.

"Good morning and thanks for the coffee," he said, taking the coffee on his way to his office.

"Good morning, boss," she said. "Don't forget, we have a meeting with that new contractor after lunch."

Jesse stopped. "We do? That's right, we do. Thanks for reminding me. Anything else?"

Nina nodded, still staring at the computer screen. "There's someone waiting in your office for you." She stopping typing and looked up at Jesse.

"Right now?" He checked his watch. "It's seven forty-five in the morning. How long has he been here?"

"Well, *she's* been here for about five minutes now. She wouldn't give me her name, but she insisted that you would want to see her."

"She?" It didn't make sense. He never made appointments this early in the day. "Is she a contractor?"

"I don't think so. At least she doesn't look like any contractor I've ever seen before. This one seems classy and beautiful," Nina answered.

"There's only one way to find out." He held up his coffee. "Thanks again for the coffee."

"You're welcome."

Jesse had no idea who could be waiting for him. A classy and beautiful woman at 7:45 in the morning? It seemed too strange. His door was open, and he saw a woman with long, curly blonde hair studying one of the designer paintings on the wall.

"Sarah?"

"No, but I often get that," the woman said, turning around. Jesse blinked a few times, but the image never changed. The woman appeared to be in her fifties, yet she looked so much like Sarah that Jesse stared. "I'm Sarah's mom, Evelyn." She held out her hand.

Jesse transferred the coffee to his left hand to shake hers. "It's a pleasure to meet you, Mrs. Ramsey."

"Please, call me Evelyn."

"I can't believe how much you look like Sarah," he said, still shaking her hand.

"I get that a lot."

He let go of her hand and gestured to the leather chair across from his desk. "Please, have a seat." He set his coffee on his desk and sat down.

"Thank you." Evelyn's dress was a lightweight silk with a floral pattern and clung to her thin frame. Jesse could see why Nina had referred to her as classy and beautiful. She walked with an easy grace that wasn't too flashy, but was definitely noticeable. He imagined that she turned heads wherever she went.

"So, what brings you here?"

"You," she answered with a smile.

Jesse instinctively smiled back. "Is there something I can do for you?"

"I hope so," she said. "You see, I have this sweet and adorable little granddaughter and she means the world to me. I'd do just about anything for her." She paused as if giving Jesse the opportunity to respond, but Jesse said nothing. "I'm afraid that what she needs the most right now is something that I can't give her."

"And what's that?" Jesse asked.

"A father."

Jesse ran his hand through his hair. *Father*, a title that he'd not yet gotten used to hearing. One that both terrified and interested him. "Mrs. Ramsey," he began.

"Evelyn," she interrupted.

"Evelyn," Jesse said, "I'm not sure if it would be wise for me to just suddenly show up and say, 'Hey Emma, it's me, your biological father.' I doubt that Sarah would like that very much either."

Evelyn sat back and crossed her legs. "I know that you and Sarah have a complicated history. But several things happened and one of those *things* was that you two had a child together. Now I know that it wasn't an ideal way of bringing a child into this world, but you did nevertheless."

"I just found out about Emma not that long ago. For all five years of her life, I never even knew that she existed. And entering her life now after all of these years would be a major step. One that can't be taken lightly."

"Sarah tried to tell you about Emma. And she and I both know that she should have done more. No one feels more terrible about that than she. But regardless, it doesn't change what's right for Emma now." She uncrossed her legs and leaned forward. "Listen, I know things have been complicated between you and Sarah. And I know that you've been through a lot lately. But all I'm asking is that you consider getting to know your daughter. She needs a father, and I *believe* that you are a good man."

"How does Sarah feel about this? And what about Kevin?" Jesse asked, sitting back in his chair.

"Kevin is not her father."

"No, but he's all Emma knows as her father."

"Which is why I feel you should be involved in her life more than ever."

"What do you mean?"

Evelyn took a deep breath. "I liked Kevin. In the beginning he did so much for Sarah, giving up his job to work for his father so that Sarah had the money to focus on

her dreams. And he's always been a very charming man."
Evelyn's compliments regarding Kevin sent tiny daggers
into Jesse's skin. "But he's really changed over the years.
In fact, I don't even recognize him anymore. Sarah's dealt
with a lot of crap from him. But enough was enough, and
she knew she had to get out. And the way Emma is around
him…well, let's just say that she prefers to stay with her
mom."

Jesse's eyes narrowed. "Is he abusive?"

She shook her head. "Not to Emma."

"Sarah?"

She nodded.

Jesse's jaw tightened and his hand curled into a fist.

"I know he's lost his job," Evelyn said. "And he's
been drinking a lot, and he hasn't exactly been dealing with
the divorce well either."

Jesse remembered the conversation he had had with
Robbie just the other day in this same office. How
concerned Robbie had sounded about Sarah. "How
dangerous is he?"

"I don't know. I just wish he'd get some help." She
paused and looked out the window for a moment. "I know
my daughter, and although she isn't perfect, she still wants
what's best for Emma. She loves her very much."

"I can see that."

"And, Jesse, I know about your parents. I know that
it must have been hard going through something like that at
such a young age. And I'm sure you've heard what kind of
a mom I was, too. You and I both know how important it is
for a child to have her parents. Even though you and Sarah
aren't together, it's still important that Emma has her

parents in her life. Both of her parents." She stood up and walked over to the door. "And, Jesse?"

"Yes."

"I want you to know one thing."

"What's that?"

"I don't know what your opinion is of Sarah, but she really cares for you. She never meant to hurt you or Kate."

Jesse let out a long sigh. "I know."

"Please think about this conversation. Emma really is a good and wonderful child." She paused and placed her hand on the side of the door. "She looks so much like you, Jesse."

Jesse smiled.

"Please don't make the same mistakes I made. Emma might find a way to forgive you someday, but you will never forgive yourself."

Chapter Twenty-eight

Sarah

Sarah picked up the phone and dialed her mother.

"Hello."

"Hey, Mom, it's me. How's Em doing?"

"She's fine. We're working on her math homework right now."

"Really? I usually have to fight with her to get her to do her homework."

"Let's just say that I have the magic touch. Did you want to speak with her?"

"Yes, please."

Sarah flipped through a magazine and scanned an article on small gardens. "Hello, Mommy." Emma's sweet voice rang through the telephone and went straight to her heart.

"Hey, Em, are you being good for Grandma?"

"Yeah. She's giving me a dollar to do my homework."

"Really?" So much for a magic touch. "That was nice of her."

"Yep. And if you pay me a dollar every time I have homework, I could have five dollars a week."

"Honey, we'll have to talk about that later. But it's good to see your math skills are improving."

"Thanks, Mommy. I miss you."

"I miss you, too. I'm going to leave work in about an hour and come get you. Okay?"

"Can we get ice cream?"

"How about we get some dinner first, and then we'll talk about the ice cream."

"Okay. I'm going to finish my homework now."

"Make sure you have Grandma check it."

"I love you, Mommy."

"I love you, sweetie."

Sarah hung up the phone and walked through the swinging doors to the front of the store. She watched as Rachael finished ringing up a few customers. "You have a nice day," Rachael said, giving her best smile. She waited for them to leave before turning to Sarah. "How's Em?"

"Good. She's doing her homework...for money." Rachael gave her a questioning look.

Sarah waved her off. "Don't ask."

"Do you mind if I slip out to grab a bite to eat? I'm starving."

"Sure. But I'll need to leave in an hour, okay?"

Rachael grabbed her purse and walked over to the front door. "I'll be back in a flash. If any cute guys walk through this door, feel free to flirt with them while I'm away." And with a ring of the bell, she left.

Sarah opened the three-ringed binder portfolio of some of her best displays and flipped through them. Then the doorbell rang again. "What did you forget?"

"I forgot to tell you how absolutely ravishing you look today."

Sarah looked up to find Kevin standing just inside the store. Something about him seemed...off. His disheveled-looking, slicked-back hair and wrinkled suit sent off alarms inside of her. But the thing that caught her eye the most was his five o'clock shadow. Never had she seen him so unkempt. Hairs on the back of her neck tingled and a chill ran down her spine. "Hello, Kevin."

He walked slowly around the store, as if walking through the park on a Sunday afternoon. "You really have done a wonderful job with this place."

"Thanks. Is there something that I can help you with?"

He shook his head. "No, I'm just here to get Emma."

"Emma? She isn't here. You said that you wanted her in two days."

Kevin continued walking through the store, drawing closer to Sarah without ever looking at her. "That wasn't our agreement. We agreed on Thursday. I remember it very clearly."

"That's right," Sarah agreed. "Today's Tuesday."

Kevin stopped, his eyes narrowed and his head cocked to the side. "No, today is…" Then a smiled formed across his face. "Today is Tuesday. I should've checked my calendar."

"If you want to come back then, she'll be ready for you."

He started walking again, this time a direct path to Sarah. "Where is she?"

"She's not here."

"You said that already. But I'm asking where she is."

"She's with my mother. Kevin, is there something wrong? You look—"

"Like shit," he interrupted her.

"I was going to say tired." The closer he got, the more sick she became.

"I'm glad you said something, Sarah dear. Because I do feel tired. So very tired these days."

Only the counter separated him from Sarah. She could smell the alcohol on his breath, and it instantly nauseated her. "Well, maybe you should go home and get some rest."

"You see, that's the problem, Sarah dear. I can't seem to get much rest these days. You, on the other hand," he motioned to Sarah, "look very rested. I think divorce suits you well. In fact, I don't think I've ever seen you look this good before."

She remembered the talk she had had with Rachael at the store while shopping for Emma. Rachael was right, she needed to stand up to him. He would never take her seriously until she did. "Speaking of divorce, Kevin." She felt the muscles in her back tense. "When are you going to sign the papers?"

Kevin placed his hand on her portfolio and turned it to face him. Then he started flipping through the papers. "I'll tell you what. You give me what I want. I'll give you what you want."

Tired of his games, she let out a sigh. "What is it that you want?"

His smile grew wider. He leaned over the counter and smelled the side of her neck. "Oh, you know what I want, Sarah dear." Her hands began trembling. "I want what you've been giving that street rat, Jesse."

"What are you talking about?"

"Don't lie to me."

"I think you should go now."

Kevin slammed his hand on the counter. "Why? Why should I go?"

"If you don't leave, I will call the cops. Now go."

Kevin smiled, turned around, and then quickly turned back to Sarah, grabbing her wrist and pulling her over the counter. "I don't think you really want me to go."

"Kevin, you're hurting me. Please, let go."

He squeezed her tighter. "You haven't felt pain yet."

She slapped him across the face, causing him to let go. He smoothed his greasy hair back into place and took a deep breath. Then he climbed across the counter, knocking down the binder and a few pens, and placed himself between her and the exit. Her heart raced and she found it difficult to breathe. He pressed his body against hers. "Don't you ever hit me like that again!" he shouted. "What gives you the right? It wasn't enough for you to leave me— abandon me. No. You had to go back to sleeping with that dirt bag, Jesse, and you're turning our daughter against me, too. Do you know how that makes me feel?!" His shouting grew louder and louder. Anger, fear, hatred, and resentment all stirred in Sarah at the same time, creating a hurricane of panic. She tried to climb over the counter, knocking over the register, but he pulled her back over, causing her back to slam against the wall, sending pictures crashing to the ground. "Now I'm going to show you exactly what it's like to lose everything. You are going to feel how I feel!" And he raised his fist.

Chapter Twenty-nine

Jesse

"I don't think so." Jesse reached across the counter, grabbing Kevin's wrist with one hand and sending his other fist careening into Kevin's face, knocking him into the wall. "That isn't how you're supposed to treat a lady, Kevin." Jesse grabbed Kevin by his jacket, and pulled him back over the counter, letting him drop to the ground. "Get out of here."

Kevin stood and collected himself without ever looking at Jesse or Sarah. Then he sent a wide right hook to Jesse's face. Jesse ducked and planted an uppercut to Kevin's stomach and a cross punch to his face. Kevin spit a mouthful of blood onto the floor. "What're you going to do, Malone? You going to take care of me the same way your father took care of your mother?"

The last bit of self-control snapped inside Jesse. He grabbed Kevin by the jacket, dragged him toward the door, then slammed him into the wall. "Leave here now and never come back."

"Jesse, if I didn't know better, I'd say that you have a lot of pent-up hostility. What's the matter? Girl problems?"

"If I ever see you around here again, I swear I'll—"

"How is that little beauty of yours? What's her name, Kate? She sounded so pleasant over the phone. How is she feeling these days? Nasty accident, by the way."

Jesse remembered what Kate had said about an anonymous caller telling her that Jesse wanted to meet at the park. It had been Kevin. Rage pumped through Jesse's veins like fire. A monster was about to be unleashed, one that he swore he'd never let out. So he let go and took a step back.

Kevin straightened his tie again. "That's more like it. Now if you don't mind, I've more important places to be. You can have her." He motioned to Sarah. "She's just trash like you."

Those words pushed a button inside Jesse. He knew then and there that Kevin could never be around Sarah or his daughter ever again. He had to protect them both. Jesse dove into Kevin, pinning him against the wall. "I'm telling you, stay away from Sarah and Emma."

Kevin bared his teeth, like a rabid dog. "Don't you ever tell me what to do when it comes to my daughter."

"Then maybe it's time you know the truth about that."

"Jesse!" Sarah shouted.

"What's he talking about?" Sarah didn't respond. Kevin turned to her. "What's he talking about?!"

She looked down, as if unable to look Kevin in the eyes.

Then Kevin looked at Jesse, as if seeing him for the first time. The same eyes he'd been looking into for the past five years. He shrank beneath Jesse's hands, like a balloon that had been deflated. Hatred and tears filled his eyes. Jesse let go and took a step back.

"All these years!" he shouted. "And you never..."
He turned to Jesse. "We'll finish this later." Then he
walked out of the store.

Jesse walked over to Sarah and wrapped his arms
around her. "Are you okay?"

She let herself go in his arms and spent the next few
minutes crying.

"It's okay." Jesse said. He waited for her stop
crying before letting go. She walked over to the counter
and started picking up the mess. Jesse bent over and helped
pick up her things. He noticed a bruise forming on her
wrist. "You should call the cops."

"Really? And then what?"

"And get a restraining order. He's out of control.
And did you smell the alcohol on his breath? I don't think
you or Emma's safe around him."

"Why did you have to tell him, Jesse?"

"I don't know. I guess I just felt like he was a threat
to your and Emma's safety. I just wanted him to stay
away."

"Listen, I know I was wrong for not trying harder to
tell you that Emma was your child. And now Emma thinks
that her father is Kevin. I know he doesn't deserve her, but
that doesn't change what she believes."

"And what about me? I am her father. Don't I have
the right to that?"

"Yes. You do. But it's not just my feelings, or
Kevin's feelings, or your feelings that we have to consider.
In the middle of this mess is an innocent, beautiful little
girl. And we need to think about what's best for her."

"Well, I'll tell you what's not best for her." Jesse pointed toward the front door. "Kevin. You don't understand, Sarah. I grew up with a monster. And that son-of-a-bitch treated me, my brother Robbie, and my mother like punching bags for years. Nothing stopped him."

"Kevin wasn't like that. Not until recently. He might…"

"Might what!? Hurt you. Or worse, hurt Emma."

Tears flowed from her eyes. "I don't know what to do."

"The only thing you can do. Protect Emma." Jesse pulled out his cell phone and gave it to Sarah. "You can start by calling the police."

***

After Sarah hung up with the police, she handed the phone back to Jesse. She walked over to the front door, locked it, and flipped the sign from OPEN to CLOSED. "Thank you, Jesse. I'm so glad you showed up when you did. I don't want to think about what would've happened if you hadn't."

"Don't think about it. Is there any place we can sit?"

She headed to the back room and Jesse followed. They sat at a small round wooden table. "Is there anyone you want me to call? Your mom? Rachael?"

She shook her head.

"I'm sorry about earlier. About what I said to Kevin. I just…"

"I completely understand. You did what any loving and caring parent would do. You protected your child."

Jesse tapped his fingers on the table. "My child," he said, smiling. "I do like the sound of it."

"Good. She could use someone like you in her life."

"I don't know about that. I don't exactly have it together."

She shook her head. "You are a good man, Jesse. She's a lucky little girl."

"That's kind of why I stopped by here." He stood up and grabbed a disposable cup from the water cooler and filled it. Then he sat down again at the table and slid the cup over to Sarah. "I want to be in her life. I know that I don't know the first thing about parenting. And she already knows Kevin as her father, but I'm willing to go as slowly as needed to be a part of her life."

Sarah smiled.

"What?"

"You."

"Me?"

"Yes, you," she said. "I spent six years wondering if you ignored my letter because you weren't sure about being a father. And then when you find out that you are, amidst all this," she held up her hands, motioning around her, "you are willing to be a father despite how complicated it can be."

"What can I say, I'm a complicated kind of guy."

"Actually, in many ways, Jesse Malone, you are. But no matter what, I am thrilled that you will be in Emma's life."

Jesse stared into Sarah's crystal blue eyes and realized that after all these years, all the times they'd been separated, and all the stuff they'd gone through, nothing could cause him to stop caring for her. Her strength, love for family, and the ability to see something in Jesse that others often did not made her an irresistible woman. "You are a great mother. I mean, you thought her biological father wanted nothing to do with her, so you tried to give her a normal home, with two parents and a nice house."

"And don't forget about the happy dog, Willow," she chimed in.

Jesse laughed. "Where is Willow anyway?"

"He's with my mom. Wherever Em goes, he goes."

"You see," Jesse said, motioning to Sarah. "That's what I'm talking about. Despite the adjustments in her life, she seems to be very happy still."

"As happy as a little girl who hates doing homework can be." Sarah tipped back the cup of water and drained it.

"Here, let me get you some more." Jesse reached for the cup and his hand touched hers. He froze and looked into her eyes. The electricity flowed like a storm of emotion between their hands. His pulse quickened, leaving him wanting more. He pulled his hand away, knowing there could never be anything between them. He loved Kate. And she loved him. Life had given him a second chance at love and nothing would keep him from following through this time. "Sarah, there's something I should tell you."

"Yes?"

"Does someone want to tell me what in the hell happened out here?" Rachael stood just inside the swinging doors, holding a greasy brown sack of food. "I went out for some Coney dogs, and I returned to this. Did a tornado come ripping through here or what?"

Chapter Thirty

Jesse

Jesse walked into his apartment. The sweet smell of Kate's perfume found his nose. He closed his eyes and took it in. Home sweet home. "I'm in the kitchen," she shouted. Jesse set his briefcase down and went into the kitchen. Kate sat on a bar stool at the kitchen counter, reading the newspaper. "So, how did it go?"

He walked up to her and placed his arms around her. "It went...okay, I think."

"Just okay?"

"Well, we talked. And she is excited about me being in Emma's life. She agrees that we should take it slowly, and gradually build into it."

Kate squeezed him back. "I'm so happy for you. And I can't wait to meet Emma."

"You're going to love her. She has the biggest blue eyes. And these tiny dimples."

"So, she's a mini version of you."

Jesse ran a hand through his hair and smiled. "She is an attractive little girl. That's for sure."

"And hopefully she got your modesty, too."

"All right, enough about me. What about you? How did your parents take your moving back in here?"

She rubbed her chin. "Let's see. My mom cried, saying that it was too soon. My father said something along the lines of it being over his dead body that he would see his little girl marrying such a *despicable* man."

"Let's look on the positive side. He still considers me a man."

She hit him on the shoulder. "Don't joke about this. At this rate, we'll have to wait fifty years before he'll be ready for us to get married."

"Hey," Jesse held up his hands in a boxing position. "You don't want to mess with me."

"Oh my gosh! You're bleeding." She grabbed his hand.

"It's nothing," he said, pulling it back.

She grabbed his hand again. "Jesse Malone, this is not nothing. It looks like you hit someone."

Jesse looked away.

"Jesse? Did you hit someone?"

"It's complicated."

"What do you mean complicated? You were just going to see Sarah and talk about being more involved in your daughter's life, not slug someone."

"It wasn't like that."

"Jesse!?"

"When I showed up, her husband, Kevin, was there and he was roughing Sarah up."

"What! I thought she was divorced."

"I guess they are going through the divorce right now. What was I supposed to do, let him hurt her?"

"No. But this doesn't sound good at all. Did you call the cops?"

"She did. That's kind of why it took so long. They wanted me to give a statement."

Kate's elbow fell to the counter and she rested her head on her hand, shaking it from side to side.

He placed his hand on her shoulder and massaged it. "What's the matter?"

"Everything. Can't you see? There's a psycho ex out there who wants to beat you up. My father can't stand the idea of us being together. My leg is broken, and it's really not a good look for me."

"I've always thought pink looked sexy on you," Jesse joked. "You remember when you wore that pink lace—"

She pinched his lips shut. "Don't. I'm being serious. What are we going to do?"

Jesse shrugged. "Tell the world to get lost."

Kate's eyes turned from smile to serious. "That's a great idea."

"What is?"

"We should get married."

"We are." He held up her hand and pointed to the ring on her finger.

"We should get married tomorrow!"

Chapter Thirty-one

Robbie

The brass bell rang when Robbie walked through the pet shop door. Ricky had a clipboard in hand, checking off the inventory of dog toys. "How's it lookin'?"

"Good, boss. I'm finishing up here and then I'm going to feed the pups."

"Don't worry about that. I'll feed 'em."

"All right." Ricky tucked a pen behind his ear. "Then I'll take care of stocking the shelves."

"How about you take a break?" As much as Robbie loved how much work Ricky did around the shop, he worried about him getting burnt out. "In fact, take a long break. You deserve it, man."

Ricky smiled. "Thanks, boss."

"And stop calling me boss. It's Robbie."

"Roger that." Ricky walked into the back room, hopefully hanging up his apron and taking a break, but with Ricky, there was no telling. The man never sat still.

Robbie filled a bucket with dog food and headed for the fur balls who were already standing with paws against the cage, yelping. "All right. All right. I've got some good grub for you guys and gals. Of course it's the same as this morning, and last night, and pretty much every other meal you've had. That reminds me, how do you guys eat the same thing day in and day out?"

"Talking to the dogs now?"

Robbie dropped the bucket of dog food, sending it rolling down the aisle. "Dang it, Jesse. You scared the crap out of me."

"I'm sorry, big brother. Are you afraid of the boogey man, too?"

Robbie pointed his food scooper at Jesse. "Hey, Ponyboy, the boogey man is nothing to joke about."

"Let me help you." Jesse crouched down and scooped handfuls into the bucket. "I wanted to stop by and apologize for the other day."

Robbie shook his head. "Don't worry about it. I was more mad at myself than you."

"Why?"

"All those years, and I had no idea what you had sacrificed for me."

Jesse looked Robbie in the eyes. "You are the one who sacrificed for me."

"What are you talkin' about?"

"You took the fall for Dad's death. Growing up, the kids thought it was you, so they went after you the most. For years, you protected me. I had the chance to get you out of that prison, and in a way, freeing you freed me. Besides, we look after each other."

Robbie looked down. Then he nodded. "You're right. I am pretty great, ain't I?" He held up one of the dog food pebbles and stared at it. "Do you remember the time when I convinced you to eat dog food? I told you that it was a new chocolatey cereal."

Jesse nodded. "Not one of my favorite memories."

"And you're supposed to be the smart one." They sat in silence picking up the rest of the dog food. A weight had been lifted from his shoulders. He hated conflict between him and Jesse. Then he noticed the scrapes on Jesse's knuckles. "So, when are you gonna tell me who you were scrappin' with?"

Jesse put his hands into his pockets. "What are you talking about?"

Robbie pointed at his pants. "I already saw your knuckles. I was a boxer, man. I know what your hands look like when you slug someone."

"It was Kevin."

"What? You punched the million-dollar smile?"

Jesse nodded. "You were right. I went to talk to Sarah about Emma and he was there, manhandling Sarah. So, I…intervened."

"Then what happened?"

"Then he left."

Robbie tapped Jesse on the shoulder. "I told you that dude was up to no good. So, what are you gonna do now?"

"Sarah and I have agreed that I should start becoming a part of Emma's life. Starting slowly and then gradually seeing her more."

"As a father of a little girl myself, I think you're doin' the right thing. Besides, Maddie is going to love having a cousin to hang out with. There aren't too many Malones around here."

"Funny you should mention family. I came here to talk to you about something else."

Robbie opened one of the cages and dropped a scoop of food inside. Something inside of him hesitated before inviting what was on Jesse's mind. He filled another scoopful of pebbles. "What's that?"

"Kate and I are getting married tomorrow."

Robbie missed the dish, sending the pebbles across the bottom of the cage. The puppies scrambled and climbed over each other to get their share. "Dang it!" He put the scooper back into the bucket.

"I thought you would be happy."

"I am happy for you. If this is really what you want to do."

"I love Kate. Why wouldn't I want to marry her?"

Robbie set the bucket down. "You guys have been through a lot lately. And I mean a lot. A marriage is hard enough without all the other…stuff added to it."

"Since when did you become Dr. Phil?"

Robbie threw up his hands. "You don't have to take my advice. All I'm doin' is lookin' out for my little brother."

"Sorry," Jesse ran a hand through his hair. "I'm just tired of roadblocks, man. I'm ready to move forward for once."

Robbie placed his hand on Jesse's shoulder. "Look at you. Through the obstacles and the storms, you're really following through this time. I was talkin' to a different Jesse just one year ago. But now," he put his hand on Jesse's head and messed up his hair, "you're all grown up."

"Yeah, and you're not doing so bad yourself." He pinched Robbie's cheek.

Robbie remembered when his Aunt Sherry used to pinch his cheeks. She would have been thrilled and proud of Jesse. Life never got her down, either. "You remember what Aunt Sherry used to say? Life seldom gives you what you want it to."

"But it gives you what you need it to. And with a little bit of hard work, your dreams become a reality."

"I miss her."

"I miss her, too. Robbie, she'd be so proud of you. The way you've handled raising Maddie on your own. And how you've grown the business, too. I wish she were here right now."

Robbie looked up at the ceiling. "She's here. If there's one thing I'm sure of, she's here. And she's smilin' down on you."

Chapter Thirty-two

Robbie

Robbie stared into the mirror and shook his head at the crooked mess of a knot he had made with his tie. "I run a pet shop. I have no idea how to tie a tie." He pulled it out and retied the knot. A little better this time, but far from good. "Why do people wear these?"

"Can I see it?"

He turned to Madison standing beside him. Her white flower-girl dress flared out at the waist, ending just above her white slipper shoes. Her curly dark hair had a flower pin, and he couldn't believe how much she looked like her mother. "You are the cutest little princess I've ever seen."

She smiled, revealing her two missing teeth. "Thank you, Daddy. You look handsome."

"I can't seem to get my tie right."

Madison pulled up a chair and stood on top of it. "Let me take a look at it." She pulled and straightened his tie. Her green eyes reflected the light the way her mother's had, leaving him missing Felicia more than ever. She would know how to fix his tie. She always knew what to do. "There."

He looked back into the mirror and smiled. "Wow, you did it. This might actually pass as a good knot."

"The girls are going to think you are so handsome."

He turned back to Madison. "The girls? Honey, I don't know if this is the type of wedding girls will be at."

184

Her shoulders sank along with her smile.

"What's the matter, baby girl?"

"Why don't you have a wife, Daddy?"

"What?"

"Like Uncle Jesse. Why don't you have a wife?"

He put his hands on her arms. "Would you be happy if I had a…wife?"

She shrugged. "I just don't want you to be lonely."

"Aw, baby girl, I'm not lonely. I have you." He pulled her into a hug. Until now he had worried about putting another woman into his life. About how Maddie would feel, sharing him with another woman. He had never thought about how it might affect her growing up without a mom. He bit back tears. "You are growin' up so fast, baby girl."

"I know. I'm taller than most of the other girls in my class."

"I bet you are." He pulled away, keeping his hands on her shoulders. "But I want you to know that no matter what, I am always going to be in your corner. You know what that means, right?"

"I think so." She looked down and bit her bottom lip. "It means that you're always going to take care of me."

"That's right, baby girl. No matter what, I will take care of you. You are the most precious thing in my life."

"I love you, Daddy."

"I love you, baby girl. You ready for a wedding?"

The brass bell rang and Robbie heard a frantic voice downstairs in the shop. "Stay right here, Maddie. I'm gonna go check on somethin'." He picked her up and set her feet on the floor. "I'll be right back."

The closer Robbie got to the pet shop, the louder the commotion grew. "Robbie's upstairs, I'll be right back." Ricky started toward the stairs when he nearly ran into Robbie.

"Ricky, what's goin' on?"

"I don't know. This woman just came into the shop. She's upset about something, but she's not making any sense to me. Something about her kid and Jesse."

"All right. Where is she?"

Ricky pointed to the entrance. "I left her at the front of the store."

"I'll go see what she wants. Why don't you man the register?"

"Okay, boss. I mean, Robbie."

Robbie went to the front door and saw the one person he never thought he'd see today. "Sarah?"

Chapter Thirty-three

Jesse

Jesse and Kate walked up the steps of the church. They stopped just before walking inside. He grabbed her hand. "This is it. You're going to walk through those doors an Ashcroft and walk out a Malone."

"You just gave me goose bumps."

"So, you're ready for this?"

She nodded. "And you?"

"No doubt in my mind. I love you."

"I love you, too."

They walked through the doors of the church. Not the church they had originally planned to get married in, but life didn't always give you what you wanted. Pastor Fifer met them at the entrance. "Hey there, kids. I hope you're not nervous. Although it would be perfectly natural if you were."

Jesse squeezed Kate's hand. "I think we're fine."

"All right. Good to hear." He pointed off to a door left of the podium. "That's where you'll be, Jesse. Your tux and everything else you requested are in there waiting for you." He pointed to a door to the right of the podium. "Kate, you'll find everything you need in there."

Jesse looked at Kate. Her eyes shone, reflecting her excitement. "I'll see you soon."

"I can't wait."

Jesse watched as Kate walked down the aisle and disappeared into the room. Then he shook the pastor's hand. "Thank you so much for doing this on such short notice."

"It's no problem. I remember when your aunt and uncle used to bring you and your brother here. You're all grown up now."

Jesse nodded. "I have a lot of good memories in this church."

"Well, I'll leave you to your room. Showtime is about an hour from now."

Jesse didn't know if it was what Pastor Fifer had said or the way he had said it, but his words ignited a flurry of butterflies inside his stomach.

When Jesse walked through the darkly stained door, he found a small room with a tuxedo hanging from a coat hook on the wall. He walked over to the tux and unzipped the plastic cover. He stared at the shiny black tux and took inventory of how surreal the moment felt.

Jesse took down the tux and, piece by piece, he put it on. The pants, white shirt, cuff links, a vest, and the final touch, a black and silver bow tie. He stood in front of the full-length mirror and buttoned his vest. Then he took a step back and weighed the image in front of him. "Not bad. A little like a butler. But what do you expect when you have to find a tux the day of your wedding?" The day had been busy. First they had to find the church, which was an easy choice for Jesse, but he'd had to convince Pastor Fifer to have a meeting with them during lunch. Once they were sure the pastor was on board, they got busy calling everybody they knew, mostly friends and a few close relatives of Kate's. Most of them said yes, and all of them sounded shocked.

Robbie had agreed to take care of the reception arrangements, the limo, and the food. At first Kate found it difficult to let go of those decisions, but when she saw her own To Do list, she realized that she had no choice.

Jesse opened the door a crack and looked out at the people gathering in the pews. Most of them were people Kate had worked with over the years. Then Jesse spied a contractor. Not one he'd worked with yet, but a new contractor he had recently hired for the Drake project. The Drake made it impossible for them to go on a real honeymoon right now. So, they had decided to do a long weekend in New York. Nothing like a five-star hotel to give you that honeymoon feel. Jesse watched as the contractor sat in the pew with his little girl, who Jesse guessed to be around seven, not much older than Emma. He wondered what she was doing at that moment. Working on her homework, eating an early dinner, or watching television. He'd lost a lot of time with her. Time he'd never get back. He shook his head. The past was the past, and nothing he did now could change it.

He closed the door and took a seat. He looked at his watch and realized how late it was getting. Where was Robbie? He pulled out his phone to call him when he heard a knock on the door. "It's about time," he said, putting his phone away. "You'd better have your suit on." He opened the door and found Kate, looking gorgeous in her floor-length wedding gown. "What are you doing here? I thought we weren't supposed to see each other yet."

"There's something I have to tell you."

"It can't wait until after?" She didn't answer. Didn't have to answer. The desperate look in her eyes said it all.

He opened the door all the way and stared as she walked inside the tiny room. Jesse shut the door behind her, finding it impossible to take his eyes off of her. "You look...gorgeous."

"Thank you." She scanned him from head to toe. "You look very handsome yourself."

"Thanks. I was thinking about wearing a tux every day. Make it the new dress code at work."

She smiled. "I'm sure the contractors would appreciate that."

Her strapless gown revealed her thin shoulders and olive-colored skin. It hugged her tiny frame down to her waist where it opened up like a giant white rose, cascading to the ground. "I can't get over how beautiful you look."

She pointed over to the two chairs in the center of the room. "Can we sit down?"

"Sure. If you can."

She ran her hands down her back, lifting up her gown as she eased into the chair. Jesse took the seat in front of her. "What's on your mind?"

"I have something I have to tell you."

"Okay. You're starting to worry me, Kate."

"When you moved to New York, I was devastated. I spent a year trying to get over you. And when I couldn't, I borrowed some money from my father to open a salon in New York. I convinced him that it was a great business opportunity. And as it turned out, it was."

"So, the real reason you moved to New York was because of me."

She nodded. "As soon as I moved there, I looked you up and asked you out to lunch. Then we started hanging out every weekend that you weren't studying, and I had this idea about us moving in together."

Jesse tried to remember the exact conversation that had led to them moving in together. They had just walked out of a movie, one he couldn't remember now, and he had been joking about sharing his room with the roaches. And it was Kate who had the idea that they should share rent, of which he would have the smaller portion since he was a full-time student, and it was all he could afford at the time. "Okay, so you wanted to be roommates."

"We were roommates for two years, and you never so much as kissed me. Every day, it was all I could think about. Just one more kiss from you. I knew if you did, you'd remember what we had in Chicago, and we'd... well, we'd be happy together."

Jesse took a deep breath, trying to process all the information, and feeling at a loss for words.

"Two years went by and nothing happened. Not a kiss, not a look, not anything that resembled more than a friendship."

"That's because I was focused on my schooling. I didn't want anything getting in the way of finishing what I had set out to do."

"That's right," Kate nodded. "But as the two years came to an end, I knew that you would either move back to Chicago or take a job in New York, but it meant that we would no longer be roommates. You'd move on and maybe even find someone else." She looked down at a tattered tissue she'd been carrying. "I didn't want to lose you."

"But what about that guy you were dating? The guy who proposed to you. Nate."

"Nate and I did go on a few dates. But he could tell that my heart belonged to someone else." She looked up at Jesse. "It belonged to you."

"And the engagement ring?"

"I paid for it. I didn't want to lose you, so I thought, what if you thought that you'd lose me to another man, that maybe it would...I don't know, trigger something inside of you. Make you realize that you wanted me."

"But I did want you. After classes were over and the exams were past me, I found myself for the first time able to think about what else I had in my life. Which was you. You didn't have to buy a ring to get me to realize that."

"I know that now." Tears welled in her eyes.

"So, is this what you had to tell me?"

"Not all of it."

Jesse's stomach coiled into a ball, nervous about what else she had yet to reveal.

"Sarah came to see me when I was in the hospital."

"She did?"

Kate nodded. "She wanted to apologize. She told me how sorry she was for the accident and what I had seen at the park. She wanted to reassure me that there was nothing going on between the two of you."

Jesse held up his hands. "There wasn't. I promise."

"I know. I believe you." She twirled the tissue in her hands. "She told me that you were one of a kind. That I shouldn't make the same mistake she'd made by letting you go."

"She did?"

Kate nodded. "Here's the thing, Jesse. You are a great man. One that any woman would be lucky to have.

One that I would be lucky to have. But there's only one woman who you were meant to have." Jesse held his breath. Every passing second felt like an eternity of waiting. Tears ran down her cheeks. "You should be with Sarah."

"Why would you say that? I love you."

"Not the way that you love Sarah. I saw the way you two looked at each other in the flower shop. I tried to push it away, but deep down inside, I knew. Then I saw again at the park when you two were about..."

Jesse grabbed Kate's hands. "That was a mistake."

"Was it?" Kate asked. "We've never looked at each other that way. With that kind of unconditional love. The type of love that lasts through anything. The type of love where the world could come crashing down around us and the one thing we'd know for sure is that nothing could destroy our love. It's like every cell in your body knows that she's the one for you and you're the one for her, even if you don't want to admit it. You're a good guy, Jesse. Which is why you would never admit it. You're willing to put my happiness ahead of your own, and I can't let you."

A lump the size of a grapefruit formed in the back of Jesse's throat, making it difficult for him to speak. "I love you, Kate."

"I could feel the love in Sarah's voice when she spoke of you. And it sounded...beautiful. I want that for myself. I deserve that, too. And as great as you are, I don't think I'll ever find that kind of love if I marry you, Jesse."

No longer able to stop them, tears rolled down Jesse's cheeks. Kate took off her ring and handed it to Jesse. "I'm sorry."

Just then, the door flew open and Robbie shot inside. "Jesse, we have a big problem."

Chapter Thirty-four

Jesse

Jesse turned around and wiped his eyes with the sleeves of his shirt. "What's going on?" Then he turned around in time to see Sarah walking in behind Robbie. "Sarah? What are you doing here?"

"Emma's missing, Jesse."

"What do you mean she's missing?"

"I waited at the bus stop to pick her up, like I do every day. The kids got off the bus, but Em never did. So, I called the school, and they said that Kevin showed up at lunch time and signed her out of school."

"So, she's with Kevin then?"

Sarah nodded. "I tried calling him, but his phone went straight to voicemail. He wasn't supposed to see her again until tomorrow, but he took her from school today. He took her, Jess." The panic in her voice caused Jesse's pulse to quicken.

"Where would he have taken her?"

Sarah looked down and shook her head. "I don't know. I tried going to his place, but the door was unlocked and no one was there. I tried the park, but nothing. I have no idea where he took her. And after yesterday, I don't know what he's going to do." Jesse remembered pure rage shooting from Kevin's eyes. "He's been drinking a lot, too. We just need to find her."

"Did you try Kevin's family, his parents, siblings, anybody he may be close to?"

"I called his parents and they haven't seen or heard from him in a week. Something's not right. And now Emma is with him. What if he left the city?"

"The first thing we need to do is call the police and report it. I don't know if they'll do anything this early into her disappearance, but we at least need to report it."

"I already called them." Sarah shifted weight to her other foot. "They're looking for her, too, but I don't know how serious they're taking it. The officer said that most of these cases end with the parent bringing the child home after spending a day at the fun park or the zoo."

Jesse turned to Robbie. "What are you thinking?"

Robbie crossed his arms. "I don't know. What was Kevin's condition when you left him yesterday?"

"I slipped and told him that Emma wasn't his child."

Robbie's arms dropped. "Are you serious?"

Jesse nodded.

"So, he's lost his job, he's lost his wife, he's been drinking, and he just found out that his little girl really isn't his little girl? We need to find Emma—now."

"All right," Jesse said. "Does anyone have a piece of paper and a pen?"

"I do." Sarah opened her purse and rummaged through it until she pulled out an empty white envelope and a ballpoint pen.

"I need you to write down ten places that Kevin and Emma have been together over the past six months to a year."

Sarah used the wall as a desk, scribing while the others stared over her shoulder. Robbie placed his hand on

Jesse's shoulder. "Don't worry, man. We're gonna find her."

Then Kate grabbed his hand and gave him a squeeze. "We'll find her."

Sarah finished and handed the envelope to Jesse. Jesse scanned the locations quickly and then tore the list in half. He handed one to Robbie. "I need you to visit these." Then he handed one to Kate. "Would you mind checking these out?"

"Not at all."

He turned to Sarah. "I need you to go back to Kevin's one more time to see if he's there. I also need you to call anyone you think he may know, friends he would turn to if he were in a crunch. Then go back to the flower shop and wait just in case he shows up."

"I'm going to check out the museum and aquarium to see if maybe he took her there." He threw on his jacket. "Sarah, make sure you have all of our cell numbers so you can let us know if you find them. That goes for all of you. When you finish your search list, go to the flower shop. If we've not found her, we will need to figure out what we're going to do next."

"What does Emma look like?" Kate asked.

"Oh," Sarah opened her purse again and pulled out her wallet. "I have some photos in here." She handed one of Emma and herself to Robbie, one of Emma and Sarah's mom to Jesse, and a photo of Emma to Kate. "These were all taken in the past few months. She went to school in a pair of blue jeans and a pink shirt with a puppy on it."

Kate studied the picture and then looked at Jesse. "She looks exactly like you."

Jesse smiled.

"So, the flower shop?" Robbie asked.

"That's where we'll meet up." Kate lifted her dress and left the room, followed by Robbie. Jesse turned to Sarah. "Don't worry. We're going to find her."

Tears rolled down Sarah's cheeks. "We have to, Jess. I don't know what I'd do…"

"Don't think about it." He wrapped his arms around her shaking body and held her tight. "She's fine. Everything is going to work out."

Sarah left the room and Jesse headed to Pastor Fifer, briefly explaining the situation. Then he turned to the people in the pews and announced that the wedding had been called off. He apologized for the inconvenience and then headed for the front door. He didn't have time to react to canceling the wedding or losing Kate. Jesse hadn't been able to be there for Emma for the past five years, but nothing would stop him from being there for her now.

Chapter Thirty-five

Sarah

After checking out Kevin's apartment again, Sarah headed over to one of his friend's houses just a few blocks away. She knocked on the door and took a step back to see if she could see any movement through the windows. A few long seconds passed when she saw a shadow pass by the window, and then the front door opened. "Hey, Sarah. I haven't seen you for a while. You want to come in?"

She shook her head. Fred had been Kevin's friend since they were in law school together. They competed over everything. Who had the best grades, then who had the nicest car, and eventually who had the biggest apartment. But beneath their boys-will-be-boys competition, they were good friends who would do anything for each other. "I can't, Fred. I need to find Kevin."

His eyes narrowed. "Are you okay?"

"Have you seen him?"

He nodded. "As a matter of fact, he stopped by yesterday. He was a little strange, too."

"What do you mean?"

"Well, I know he's under a lot of pressure with losing his job and everything, but he looked…devastated." Sarah knew that losing his job at his father's firm meant being exiled by his family. For most people it was losing a job, but for Kevin, it was like losing everything.

"What did he say?"

Fred leaned on the door handle and looked up as if trying to recall the exact conversation. "He really didn't say much. I remember that he looked terrible. Like someone had beaten the crap out of him, but I could tell that he'd been drinking and thought it had to do with that."

"But what did he say?" Impatience rang in her voice.

"I don't know. Something about how sorry he was for not being a better friend. For not being there for me when my mother died. I don't know. He wasn't making much sense. Then he handed me this." Fred pulled a gold ring from his pocket. It was a ring that Kevin's grandfather had given him, and one of the few things he owned besides his Lexus that held any sentimental value. "I asked him what it was for, but he just smiled at me and said it was for answering the door. But I didn't know what that meant."

Sarah did. For Kevin's family, image was everything. He didn't have any siblings or close cousins. He didn't have time for many friends. His mom and dad were the only ones in his life he saw on a regular basis, but even then they were a cold and closed off family. And now, they probably wouldn't answer the phone if Kevin did call them. "Anything else?"

He shook his head. "Is Kevin in trouble? I know his parents are kind of controlling, but if he needs anything, tell him that he can come to me."

She nodded. "I'll tell him."

Fred shut the door and Sarah turned toward the stairs. She heard the door open behind her again and turned around. "I just remembered something else he said to me that I thought was strange. But like I said, he was drunk and saying a lot of weird stuff."

Sarah's heart raced as she waited.

"He said that he was about to beat me one more time. I asked him what he meant by that, and he smiled and said, 'I'm going to become more famous than you, Fred.' "

Chapter Thirty-six

Jesse

Sweat dripped from Jesse's brow as he hurried through the busy aquarium. It seemed that every brown-haired, blue-eyed girl was here today. He showed Emma's picture to a few of the people there, asking if they had seen his little girl. And some of the patrons gave him a disapproving look, which he really couldn't blame them for. A man in a tux running through the aquarium, looking for a little girl. As weird as it sounded to him, he knew it must be even stranger from the outside looking in, but he didn't care. Kevin had Emma somewhere, and he had to find her. His little girl.

He left the aquarium discouraged. The museum had been strike one, making the aquarium strike two. Maybe Kevin had taken her out for some ice cream, but where? There had to be at least a thousand ice cream shops just on the north side of the city alone, making the task akin to looking for a needle in a haystack. Instead, he chose to go back to the flower shop and see if the others were there yet. See if they had found anything else out.

When he arrived, lights illuminated the inside, but the sign read CLOSED. He told the cab driver to drop him off in the front and paid him. When he reached the glass doors, Willow greeted him. His fuzzy tail wagged side to side like a hyper windshield wiper.

Sarah walked up behind the dog, unlocked the door, and opened it. "Willow, get back. Let him in."

"I went to the museum and the aquarium, but I didn't see them there."

"I went to Kevin's, but it was still the same. Door unlocked and it didn't look like anyone had been there for a while. So, I went to a friend of his, Fred. He did see Kevin yesterday, and he said that he could tell he'd been drinking and he was saying some strange stuff."

Willow walked up to Jesse and sniffed his pants. "What else did he say?"

"Something about how he was going to be famous." She placed a hand on Jesse's arm. "Jesse, I'm so worried. What if he does something completely stupid? What if he hurts Emma?"

"He's not going to. He may be upset that he's not her real father, but he won't hurt her. Besides, she's the same little girl that he's loved and taken care of for the past five and a half years."

Willow sniffed Jesse's hands with his cold, wet nose. Jesse wiped his hands on his pants.

"I just want her home."

"I know. So do I." He looked around the store. "Has anyone else shown up?"

"No, you're the first."

"They shouldn't be much longer."

Willow jumped up on Jesse, causing him to fall back a step. "Hey, Willow. I missed you, too."

"Willow, no. Get down." Sarah grabbed him by his collar and pulled back to get him off of Jesse. "I'm sorry about that."

"It's okay. I still can't get over how big he's gotten. He's a horse."

"I sometimes think Emma believes he is one. She's tried to ride him a few times. But he never liked it much."

"I can see why." Jesse got down on one knee and rubbed behind Willow's ears. His eyes closed and his head turned to the side. Then his back leg released a few kicks. "Feel good, buddy? Yeah. I bet you miss Emma, don't you."

"They are inseparable." Sarah crouched down and rubbed Willow's soft belly. "He's a good dog."

Jesse remembered when he had given Willow to Sarah. The look on her face when she'd seen the puppy. How happy she'd been that day. Then he remembered Dr. Bradtmiller stopping by and giving her a letter written by her father before he'd passed away. The letter that led them to the time capsule and her mother's ring buried beneath the willow tree back in New Haven. The same night they had conceived Emma.

Willow turned sideways, knocking Sarah onto Jesse. "Sorry. He forgets how big he is."

"That's okay." Jesse stood up and pulled out his phone. "I'm going to check in with Robbie."

Just then the bell chimed as the front door opened. "Did you guys find anything?" Robbie asked, winded.

"Not much. They weren't at the museum or the aquarium. What about you?"

Robbie took a few deep breaths before responding. "I checked all the parks on the list. Then I checked Millennium Park across the street." He shook his head. "Nothing." Then he looked around. "Where's Kate? Have you heard from her?"

"Not yet. She should be here anytime now."

Ten minutes went by before Kate arrived. She had struck out, too. They all looked at Jesse, who had been pacing up and down the store trying to figure out what to do next.

"Sarah, what is Emma's favorite thing to do? If you picked her up from school and asked her what the one thing she'd like to do today was, what would she say?"

"She'd want to—" The phone rang, interrupting her.

Chapter Thirty-seven

Sarah

Everyone froze and stared at the counter where the phone sat next to the register. She looked at Jesse. He nodded. All four walked over to the phone and held their breath while she answered. "Hello, Flowers of Chicago, can I help you?"

"It's not me that needs help." Her eyes lit up from the sound of his voice and her heart sank to her stomach. She looked at the others and nodded. Jesse drew closer and Sarah placed the phone between them.

"Hello, Kevin. Where's Emma? Can I talk to her?"

"I don't think that's such a good idea."

"Let me talk to my daughter."

"Why should I? After all, you wouldn't let me see her."

"That's not true. I just wanted you to schedule it. That's what divorced people do, Kevin."

"Schedule it? Make an appointment to see my own daughter? That doesn't sound much like a partnership to me. Sounds more like a dictatorship."

"So, you're saying that you'd like to see her more? And you don't want to have to schedule time with her? That's fine, Kevin. We can work this out. What do you say we meet so that I can see her now?"

Jesse nodded in approval.

"Don't you dare patronize me, you controlling, manipulative bitch. Ever since we got married, you've been trying to control the situation. Well, you're not in control now. I am." His voice remained eerily calm.

"Then what do you want me to do?"

Kevin didn't respond. She heard nothing but his breathing on the other end.

"What do you want me to do?" she asked again.

"I'm thinking."

Sarah listened carefully for any sound or sign that told her that Emma was okay, but the only sound she heard was his breathing.

"Okay. I'll tell you what. Let's make a deal. Is that dirtbag with you now?"

She looked at Jesse and he shook his head.

"No."

"Liar!" he yelled.

"I mean, yes, he's here, but he doesn't have to go with me. I can meet you alone if you want me to."

"No, I definitely think Jesse should be there. After all, he is half responsible for this adorable little girl who I've invested so much of my own love in. But that was a lie, too."

"Kevin, listen to me. She is your little girl, too. You are the only father she knows. She loves you very much."

"Really? Is that why she'd rather stay home with you instead of visit her father? Is that why she's never really loved me the way I see other little girls love their fathers?"

"That's not true. You've always worked so much, and you were gone from us so much. Emma just didn't get to spend the time with you that she needed."

"Lies, lies, lies! You lie to me one more time and I swear, I'll hang up this phone and you'll never see either of us again."

Sarah took a deep breath to calm the nerves in her stomach. She tried to think of what she should say, anything that would make him bring Emma back home to her unharmed. "Kevin, where do you want us to meet you?"

"Oh, I don't know. You guys look so cozy inside the flower shop. Maybe I'll just come join you, instead."

Chapter Thirty-eight

Jesse

Jesse and Sarah turned to the front entrance and saw Kevin standing on the other side of the glass doors, a chrome-plated pistol in one hand and Emma in the other. He tapped the pistol against the glass, inviting himself inside. Willow came running from the back of the store, barking at the glass. Rage and panic settled at the bottom of Jesse's gut. He quickly walked over to the door, but Kevin held up the gun, pointing it right at him, and took a few steps inside the shop, pushing Jesse back. Kate gasped from behind him.

"You must be Kate." Kevin looked at Jesse. "She's pretty. What is it about you? You have no money, no power, the IQ of a salad, but girls seem to like you. Is it the eyes? The hair?" He looked down at Emma. "The same eyes and hair that I fell in love with five years ago." He looked back up at Jesse. "Deceiving eyes."

Willow lowered his head and his lips curled, baring his teeth. He growled at Kevin, echoing how Jesse felt. Kevin aimed his gun at Willow and pulled back the hammer. Jesse readied himself for the shot. "I always hated that stupid dog."

"Willow!" Sarah yelled. But he didn't back down.

"Willow!" Jesse snapped. Willow let out a few whimpers as he walked over to Sarah and sat by her side.

"Why don't you put the gun down?" Jesse asked. "We can just talk."

"Déjà vu, isn't it, Jesse. Standing here with a shiny pistol pointed right at your face. I knew I should have killed you that day in your apartment six years ago, when I found out about you and Sarah. None of this would be happening if I had." He looked at Sarah. "I'd have my wife, my little girl, but now…I have nothing." He turned back to Jesse. "I was weak then. But now I'm not."

"Kevin, please," Sarah pleaded. "Look at our little girl. Look at Em. She's scared." Emma had tears running down her cheeks. Kevin's hand locked onto her shoulder like a set of handcuffs she couldn't break free from.

Adrenaline flooded through Jesse's veins, causing his heart to beat harder and harder. He wanted to rip Kevin's arms off and beat him with them. Emma, his defenseless little girl, stood trapped in the hands of a monster, just like his mother when Jesse was twelve years old. And again, he felt helpless.

"I see that look in your eyes, Jesse. The same look you had the first time we met. You wanted to beat me up then, didn't you? But you couldn't." Kevin waved the gun back and forth. "Just like now."

"Daddy, please, let me go," Emma pleaded.

But Kevin refused to look at her, refused to acknowledge her, as if doing so would threaten the monster within. Tears rolled down Sarah's cheeks. "Please, Kevin. I'll do anything. Just let her go. Take me instead if that's what you want."

"Now why would I want you? You've been slumming it with poverty over there." He motioned his gun toward Jesse. "I don't want to catch fleas. No, I don't think so."

"What do you want?" Sarah yelled.

Kevin's smile finally made its presence. "That's simple, Sarah. I want you to suffer. I want you to suffer the same way I've suffered. I want you to lose every little thing you love. Everything you care about. And then…I want you to pay."

Chapter Thirty-nine

Robbie

Robbie knew he had to do something. Jesse and Sarah would never be able to talk sense into Kevin; they were the two he blamed. Kate, well, she was just an innocent bystander in the wrong place at the wrong time. But Robbie's criminal past had calloused him. He had been here before. A gun in his face, nowhere to run, his mortality separated only by a trigger and a bullet. He took a deep breath and then a step forward.

Kevin's eyes grew large and he pointed the gun at Robbie. "Hey, big guy, what are you doing back there?"

Robbie put up his hands. "Relax, man. I only want to talk to you."

"Well, I've got nothing to say to you. This is a family matter. Between me and these two."

"Ah, see, that's where you're mistaken. I am family. That skinny guy over there," he pointed to Jesse, "is my little brother. And I promised our aunt that I'd take care of him."

"I already know he's your brother. And I don't care."

Robbie took another step closer. "You keep coming forward and you're going to be the first to fall down. And don't think you'll be getting up this time, champ."

"So, you do know who I am." Robbie took another step forward, placing himself next to Jesse. "Well, I know who you are, too."

"You have no idea who I am."

Robbie looked at Emma. Her large blue eyes full of fear melted his heart. He thought about Madison and how angry he'd be if it were his own daughter in the hands of that greasy-haired monster. "I have an idea." Robbie paused, waiting to see if Kevin would object. "Why don't you let Emma go? She can go to the back of the store and out of the way. She can't hurt you, so she's not a threat."

"I don't think so."

"Come on, man, be smart about this. Are you really going to be able to shoot straight with an arm holding on to a little girl? Besides, she has nothin' to do with this. She didn't choose her parents, she was just born, man."

Kevin looked down at Emma, his eyes seeming to soften a bit.

"Look at her. She's innocent, man."

"Nobody's innocent."

"I have a little girl myself, and if there's one thing I know for sure, it's that Emma loves you."

Kevin stared at Emma. He kept his gun on Robbie, and he leaned down. "I'm sorry, honey." Then he let her go. Emma let loose with the tears, as if finally able to break down.

"Emma, sweetheart," Robbie said. "Why don't you take your dog into the back room."

She ran over and wrapped her arms around Sarah. "Oh, sweetie, I missed you," she said, squeezing Emma tightly. "I need you to be a big girl and take Willow into the back. Can you do that for me?"

"I don't want to leave you, Mommy," she cried.

"Shh, baby, it's going to be okay." She wiped the tears from Emma's cheeks. "I'll come get you in just a little while, okay?"

Emma nodded and grabbed Willow by the collar. "Come on, Willow," she said, patting her leg. Then they both disappeared into the back room.

Robbie looked at Jesse who shot him a thank you look. He turned to Kevin. "All right. All right. Thank you for doing that."

"Despite what you think, I'm not a monster."

"I know. I know. In fact, I know a lot about what you're goin' through."

Kevin waved his gun in his face. "You have no idea what I'm going through. Someone like you couldn't possibly understand."

"I understand more than you realize, man." Robbie lowered his hands.

"What are you doing?"

"Nothing. Just tryin' to talk to you." Robbie took another step forward.

"You take one more damn step forward and your little brother will be wearing your brains."

"All right." Robbie took a step back.

"You say you know me. Well, I know you, Robbie Malone. I know you like to play with knives. And you're pretty good with one, too."

Robbie had to check the rage boiling inside. Getting angry now served no one in a situation like this. "You're hurting inside, Kevin. I can hear it. Those insults, that's not you. That's your pain."

"Stop it with that psychobabble bullshit."

"You think I don't know you, right?"

Kevin looked around the room, as if looking for something. "That's right."

"I do, man. You're angry, you're pissed off, you hate everything and everyone, and you should, because everyone you love has let you down. Betrayed you. Bit the hand that has graciously fed them."

Kevin turned back to Robbie, but said nothing.

"And here you are now. Alone, feelin' like there's no way out. But there is a way out, Kevin. I've been where you stand now. At the end of a rope with nothin' but darkness below you."

"That's a great story. Real tearjerker."

"I know how far you're willing to go for your little girl, Kevin. I was in your shoes once before. Why do you think I turned to stealing? I wanted to provide a better life for my little girl. But instead, I found myself in a tiny cell with nothin' but self-pity. Then someone walked into my life and saved me. Changed my life forever."

"Let me guess. Your fairy godmother?"

"That someone was you, Kevin."

Kevin's head cocked to the side. "What are you talkin' about?"

"I was sittin' in a prison cell staring down the barrel of ten to fifteen years, until you came along and set me free."

Kevin pointed his gun at Jesse. "That's because of a deal I made with him."

"Are you the one who negotiated the charges down? Are you the one who made it possible for me to walk out of the cell without serving any time?"

Kevin nodded.

"Then you are the one I owe everything to. You gave me my life back. And now all I want to do is give your life back to you. All you have to do is put the gun down."

Kevin stared at the gun and then back at Robbie. Tears welled in Kevin's eyes.

"Let me help you the way you helped me. Let me give you your daughter back, the way you gave me mine. She loves you, man. That's all you need in this life. Trust me. I know."

The tears rolled down Kevin's cheeks, falling onto the hardwood floor. He lowered the gun, and Robbie allowed himself to take a breath.

Ding! The glass door chimed behind them. Rachael came walking through the door, startling them all. Robbie saw the gun come back up, pointed at Jesse. Robbie closed his eyes and slammed into Kevin. He fell onto him, and then he heard the shot.

Chapter Forty

Jesse

Jesse opened his eyes to a bright light, causing him to instantly close them. He held up a hand and opened his eyes again. Pain tore through his head like a sledgehammer smashing into concrete. "Where am I?"

"You're in the hospital."

Jesse squinted to make the blurriness fade and the world around him come back into focus. He saw someone sitting in a chair next to his bed. Her long blonde hair was the first thing he saw, followed by her soft blue eyes. "Sarah?"

"How do you feel?"

He rubbed his eyes. "Like I just got hit by a truck. What happened?"

Sarah leaned forward, placing her hands on the side rails. "You took a pretty good blow to the head."

He reached up until his fingers found the bandage on his head. "How did this happen?"

"What's the last thing you remember?"

The chair at the end of his bed held a tuxedo jacket. "I was getting married. I think. No...no, Kate said she didn't want to."

"Do you remember what happened next?"

"Robbie. He came busting into the room. Upset about something." Jesse closed his eyes, wanting desperately for the hammer to cease. And then it hit him. "Emma. He said Emma was missing." The memory unfolded in his mind, like a tape playing for the first time, having recorded time he had lost due to the trauma and head injury. The museum, the aquarium. Kevin had taken his little girl, and no one could find them. "Where's Emma?"

"She's fine. She's with my mom in the waiting room."

Jesse sat back in his bed. "Thank goodness. How did…" He remembered Kevin showing up with a gun. His pulsed raced on the monitor, beeping faster and faster.

"You should try to relax, Jesse."

He looked around the room. "Where's Kate? Is she okay?"

Sarah nodded and then tucked a strand of hair behind her ear.

"What's wrong? You always do that when you're upset."

She placed her hand on Jesse's arm. "Kevin showed up at the flower shop. He had a gun."

Jesse nodded. "I know. What happened?"

Tears welled in her eyes. "Robbie talked to him. Got him to release Emma. And almost got him to put down his gun. But then Rachael walked through the door." A tear escaped from her eye, rolling slowly down her cheek.

Jesse looked around. "Where's Robbie?"

"He pushed you aside, but when the gun went off…" She started to cry.

Jesse panicked. "What happened? Where's Robbie?"

"The bullet went into his heart," Sarah sobbed. "He died instantly."

Jesse choked on the lump growing in the back of his throat. His vision blurred once again, but this time from his own tears. The ache in his head had been replaced by a broken heart. His brother, his family, the one person who had been in his corner his entire life was gone, and no amount of medicine could fix a break like that.

***

Jesse got out of bed, against his doctor's orders. Sarah stood at his side, balancing him, the way she had done when he was a kid beneath their willow tree. His shelter from the darkness and storms that ripped through life, not caring who they destroyed. "Where is she?" he asked.

"She's right over there." Sarah pointed to her mother, sitting in a waiting room chair with two little girls in her lap. "Are you sure about this?"

Jesse's jaw tightened as he forced back the tears. He nodded. "I have to."

She helped Jesse over to the waiting area where a curly-haired girl with green eyes saw him. She sat up and yelled, "Uncle Jesse!" Then she leapt from Sarah's mom's lap and ran over to Jesse, nearly knocking him over.

"Hey, Peanut. How're you doing?"

"I fell asleep." She pointed to the bandage on Jesse's head. "Are you okay?"

"Yeah, Peanut. I'm fine." He crouched down and wrapped his arms around her, never wanting to let go. Not for fear of losing her, but because he feared what he knew he had to do. And he knew that nothing in her life would ever hurt her the way he was about to.

She pulled back and smiled. "I'm so glad you're here now." She looked around. "Where's Daddy?"

Jesse pushed a few curls from her face. "That's what I need to talk to you about. Your daddy..." He paused, keeping the tears at bay. "Daddy isn't here, sweetie."

"Where is he? Can you call him on your phone?"

Jesse shook his head. "No, Peanut. Where your daddy's at now, you can't call him. You see, your daddy passed away."

The light in her eyes faded. "He's gone?"

"Yes, baby."

Her green eyes shone with tears that filled until they could no longer hold them. Jesse brought her into his arms. "I'm so sorry, Peanut. I wish there was something I could do."

"He said he would always be in my corner. He said that."

Jesse held in his arms the one thing Robbie had cherished the most. He didn't know what to say or what to do. He held her as she cried and did the one thing he could...He simply loved her.

Chapter Forty-one

Jesse

Leaves painted in bright hues of red and orange reminded Jesse of a Terry Redlin painting. The deep blue sky made for the perfect canvas. He took in the autumn air and looked down at the little girl walking next to him. Dark curls swirled past her shoulders and her dimples deepened as she smiled up at Jesse. He had spent every day with her since Robbie's death the month before, and he knew her well enough to recognize the nervous smile she was revealing now. He gave her hand a reassuring squeeze.

When they approached the pet shop, Jesse stopped and knelt down beside Madison. "You don't have to do this if you don't want to."

She looked up at the store and Jesse could see the white stenciled lettering reflecting in her green eyes. "I'm okay."

Jesse smiled. "Of course you are." He stood up, grabbed the handle, and took a deep breath before opening the door.

The tiny brass bell rang, sending a thousand memories and feelings rushing through Jesse. This time he felt Madison squeeze his hand. They walked inside and Jesse took in the sounds of puppies barking, fish tanks bubbling, and kittens meowing. Ricky came from between two aisles. "Ricky!" Madison shouted. She let go of Jesse's hand and took off in a full sprint toward him, nearly tackling him as she plowed into his legs, wrapping her arms around him.

"Hey there, Maddie. I've missed you."

"I've missed you, too," she replied.

Jesse hadn't realized how much Ricky looked like Robbie until now. They had the same closely shaven head, strong shoulders, and arms with tattoos painted across them. Ricky looked at Jesse and nodded. Then he knelt down next to Madison. "You know who else has missed you?"

She shook her head. "Who?"

"The puppies. In fact, they were telling me yesterday how much they missed you feeding them."

Madison's eyes narrowed. "Puppies can't talk."

Ricky feigned a look of shock. "Are you kidding me? Of course they can talk. You simply have to know how to speak their language."

She looked back at Jesse. "Can I see the puppies?"

Jesse nodded. "Of course you can, Peanut."

Madison ran to the back of the store, and Jesse could hear the puppies going crazy fighting for her love and attention.

Jesse held out his hand. Ricky looked at it briefly, then drew Jesse in for a hug. "Sorry, man, but you are the closest thing I have to family."

Jesse felt a lump in his throat as he realized that Ricky was the closest thing he had to family now, too. "I know what you mean." He looked around at the store and tried to think of something else, anything else. "The store looks good. You've really done a great job."

Ricky followed his line of sight. "Thanks. I've been working more lately. You know, trying to cover for…well, you know. Besides, it's been good for me. I need to stay busy."

"I hear you," Jesse said.

"I bet you've been pretty busy, too."

"Yeah. We're both trying to adjust to everything. It's hard."

"I couldn't imagine. But I can tell you this much. She's just as lucky to have you as you are to have her."

Jesse looked down and clenched his jaw, trying to hold back the tears. "I don't really know what I'm doing."

Ricky placed a hand on his shoulder. "I've never been a father, Jess. But if there's one thing I'm certain of, it's that you are going to be a great dad. You and Robbie share the same big heart. All you have to do is love her and everything will work out."

"Thanks, man." Anger and sadness filled Jesse's veins as he wrestled with the guilt and grief of losing Robbie. Why had Robbie pushed him out of the way? He didn't owe Jesse anything. And he had that beautiful little girl to raise. Why had he taken the bullet for him?

"I have someone coming in to watch the store in about an hour so that I can check out the Lincoln Park location. But I think everything's fine over there. I've been trying to split my time between the two stores, and so far, no problems."

Jesse nodded. "Sounds good."

"Is there anything I can do for you?" Ricky asked.

Jesse reached into his pocket and pulled out a key. "As a matter of fact, there is."

"What's that?" Ricky asked. Jesse tossed the key to Ricky who caught it, his eyes narrowing as he looked down at it. "What's this for?"

"It's yours now."

Ricky shot Jesse a look of confusion. "What is?"

"Sam's Pet Shop. Both locations. They're all yours now."

"Are you serious?"

Jesse put his hand on Ricky's shoulder. "I don't have a use for this place. In fact, I don't know what I'd do with it anymore. I have enough on my plate as it is."

"I don't know what to say."

"You don't have to say anything. You and Robbie were the backbone of this place." Jesse scanned the store. "I know you'll do a great job."

"I can pay you for it. I mean, I don't have much now, but in time I can pay you—"

"No," Jesse interrupted him. "You've earned this already. Besides, this is what Robbie would have wanted."

Ricky's eyes welled. He wiped away the tears before they rolled down his cheeks. "Robbie was always like a brother to me, Jess. And as far as I'm concerned, so are you."

Jesse smiled and gave Ricky another hug. "Do me one favor though."

"Name it. Whatever you want."

Jesse looked over at Madison. "I'd like to bring Madison in every now and then to play with the puppies. I think it would be good for her."

Ricky smiled. "The puppies would love that. And so would I."

"Thanks." Jesse turned toward the stairs that led up to Robbie's apartment. "I need to take care of a few things up there. Do you mind watching Madison for me?"

Ricky shook his head. "Take your time. We'll be fine down here."

Jesse walked up the stairs and into Robbie's apartment. It looked about the same as when he had lived in it before moving to New York, although Jesse's old bedroom to the left had since been divided into two rooms, one for Robbie and one for Madison. It was a quaint little apartment that matched the pet store below.

Jesse had spent a few minutes there three weeks ago to gather a few of Madison's things. It had been too soon to do anything with Robbie's belongings. The wound was still fresh, and he didn't think he could handle it.

Jesse walked over to Robbie's bedroom, questioning if he had it in him now, and slid open the pocket door. The old wooden floor squeaked as he walked inside. A queen-size bed took up half the bedroom, and a short, out-of-place dresser stood against the wall. He walked over to the closet and found a leather-bound notebook with the word PHOTOGRAPHS on the cover.

He took a seat on the edge of Robbie's bed and opened the book. The first page had only one picture. Felicia. She was lying on a blanket at a park with one hand on the pregnant bump on her stomach. Robbie had loved her more than anything else in the world. She had changed him without trying. There was something about her that had brought out the absolute best in him.

Jesse flipped the page and saw a picture of Robbie, Kate, and Madison standing outside the entrance to the zoo.

Jesse had taken the picture, and all three were making goofy faces at him. He smiled sadly, thinking of Kate.

Two weeks earlier, she had moved to New York. She wanted a fresh start, she'd told him. To finish what she had started there years earlier, to conquer the Big Apple. But Jesse suspected that she had needed to get away from all the reminders Chicago held for her: the life they'd shared together, the love she'd lost, and the tragedy that had followed. The funny thing about fresh starts was that they were hard to do when you were in the same old place.

He remembered the day she had walked into that little room in the church, shocking him with her words as she gave him back her engagement ring. She had said, *I could feel the love in Sarah's voice when she spoke of you. And it sounded...beautiful. I want that for myself.*

Time often brought confusing moments into focus. And now, just a month later, Jesse could see how right she had been. He had loved her, but not the way she needed him to. She deserved so much more.

Jesse turned to another page and stopped when he saw a picture of Madison as a newborn. He stared at the photograph and tried to think of how Robbie must have felt that day. "You were a great dad," he said out loud. The lump in the back of his throat made its way higher. He tightened his jaw to stop the tears, but it was no good. Robbie was gone and now this beautiful little girl was going to have to face life without either of her parents. A tear fell on the photo album.

"Are you okay?"

Jesse looked up and saw Sarah standing in the doorway.

Chapter Forty-two

Sarah

Sarah wanted nothing more than to put her arms around Jesse. To absorb some of the pain that she knew consumed him. "I'm sorry for letting myself in. Ricky said it was okay."

Jesse wiped his eyes and set the book on the bed next to him. "It's okay. I was going to try to pack up some of this stuff. But I don't know what to do…" He paused and looked back at the photo album. "I don't know what to do," he said again.

"I can leave if you want."

"No. I'd like it if you'd stay. That is, if you want to."

Sarah smiled and took a few steps inside. "Emma's downstairs playing with Madison. They're covered in puppies."

"Oh good," Jesse said. "I'm sure she'll be trying to talk you into taking one home before you leave."

"I know. I fully expect that." Sarah scanned the dimly lit room. "How's Madison doing?"

"She's fine. I think. I'm still trying to figure her out. You know?"

Sarah nodded. "I bet she's trying to figure you out, too."

"That won't be too tough. How's Emma been?"

"Pretty good, all things considering."

"Yeah. I'm sorry to hear about Kevin. Given all that happened, I still don't think he meant to shoot anyone. I think the situation spun out of control. Probably more than he thought it ever would."

Sarah took a deep breath. She still remembered the call she'd received from the police two days after Kevin had shot Robbie.

"Is your husband Kevin Dawson?"

She had hesitated before answering. *"Yes. Have you found him?"*

"We believe so, ma'am. But we're sending a car for you."

Sarah had imagined Kevin sitting in a prison cell, handcuffed, demanding that they let him out of there. She simply didn't want to deal with him. Not after what had happened to Robbie. *"Is there a problem?"* she asked.

"We need you to identify the body, ma'am."

"Did the police ever find out what happened to him?" Jesse asked, bringing Sarah back to the present.

Sarah shook her head. "Not really. They found him in the Chicago River. They said that he had fallen on the bad side of some people you don't ever want to make mad. But they also said that he had enough booze in his system to fill an entire bar. So it could have been an accident, or...or suicide."

Jesse rubbed the back of his neck. "I still can't believe all that's happened. It's..."

"Crazy." Before the shooting, Kevin had lost everything. His job, his wife, his family. But it wasn't until he found out that Emma wasn't really his daughter that he broke. It was all more than he could handle. In the end, he had taken Robbie's life and maybe his own.

An uncomfortable wave of silence rolled through the room. "We were heading to the store to pick up a costume for Halloween," Sarah said, hoping to change the subject.

"Oh no." Jesse massaged his temples. "I totally forgot about getting a costume for Maddie."

"It's all right, you still have a few days before the big event."

Jesse shook his head. "I feel so…"

"Overwhelmed?"

"That's one way to put it."

"Welcome to parenting. Things never really go as planned. It doesn't matter how long you do it." She knew that her words would do little to comfort him. Defeat filled his face. She placed a hand on his shoulder. "It's going to be okay."

Jesse flashed a smile. "Thanks."

"No problem." She tucked a strand of hair behind her ear. "I thought it might be good to stop here on our way. I thought Emma might like to see the puppies."

"Kids really do enjoy this place. Does she like animals?"

"She loves them. She keeps asking me if we can get a tiger. I don't know where she got that idea, but she won't let it go."

"Stubborn?" Jesse smiled. "I'm afraid she got that from my side of the family." He stood up and put his hands in his pockets.

Sarah couldn't help but notice how good he looked in his form-hugging, dark blue T-shirt and blue jeans. "As long as she has your heart," she said.

Jesse looked down. "I don't know. I think she would be pretty lucky to have yours."

"Well, she definitely has those big blue eyes of yours." Like gravity pulling her to the earth, she took a few steps toward him.

"Have you given some thought to what we talked about the other day?"

"About you spending time with Emma?" Sarah asked.

Jesse nodded. "Yeah. I'd really like to be a part of her life."

"Of course, and I think it's a great idea. She'd be lucky to have you in her life. We'll just need to figure out the best way to start."

"I understand," Jesse said. "And I'm not trying to rush it. I know she's been through a lot already."

Sarah saw the book on the edge of the bed. "Is that a photo album?"

Jesse picked up the leather-bound book and handed it to her. "There are some cute ones of Madison in there."

She took a seat on the bed, Jesse perching beside her. "Oh my gosh. Madison definitely has Felicia's eyes."

Jesse nodded.

Sarah flipped through the pages slowly, taking in the photos like a good book, each one telling the story of Robbie and Madison. Most were only of Madison, which made sense since Robbie was the one taking the photographs. Sarah stopped when she reached the one of

Robbie bent over tying her shoe. The smile on Madison's face said it all as she looked down at him. He was her hero. Sarah bit back tears as she turned the page. Then she noticed Jesse standing up and turning away. "Are you okay?"

He turned around, tears welling in his eyes. "He died saving my life, Sarah. If he hadn't..." He ran a hand through his hair. "He'd be here now and she'd have a father. A hero. The one person who'd been there for her since the beginning."

Sarah heard what he said and felt the tension building in his voice. She placed a hand on his shoulder. She knew that if anyone could understand what Madison was going through, it was Jesse. He had grown up without his parents and even watched as his mother was violently taken from him. He knew. And with a heart as large as Jesse's, it was an amplified emotion he was reliving. "Madison will always remember how great her father was. Nothing can take that away. But she's lucky to have you, Jess."

"He wasn't supposed to die. We took care of each other. That's what we did. Now I've lost my brother and for the first time in my life I feel so...so alone."

She placed her hand on the side of Jesse's face. His bright blue eyes reflected light from the tears. She brought him into her arms and held him while he sobbed, finally letting go. "It's going to be okay," she said.

Jesse stepped back, wiping his eyes and cheeks. "I'm sorry. I'm sure you didn't come here for this."

"It's fine." She placed her hand on his shoulder. "I miss him, too."

Jesse forced a smile and took a deep breath as he looked at a photograph of Madison. "I have no idea what I'm doing. I don't know the first thing about raising a child. I don't know what I'm supposed to say to her or what I'm supposed to do."

"You're already doing it. You're loving her, and you're taking care of her. That's what she needs the most." Sarah smiled. "But I do know something else that you can do."

"What's that?"

"Come with us, and we can get her a costume, too."

Jesse looked around the room. "I can't. I still have so much more to do around here."

A pang of disappointment filled Sarah's chest. "Are you sure?"

Jesse nodded. "Yeah. I appreciate the offer though."

"If you need anything, don't hesitate to call."

"Thank you. For everything."

Sarah walked out of Robbie's old apartment and turned to Jesse one last time before shutting the door. She wanted more than anything to put her arms around him. To feel his strength and love the way she had all those years ago. But things were different now. Jesse and Sarah were different now.

Chapter Forty-three

Jesse

Dark clouds filled the sky, blocking most of the sunlight. The wet ground from days of rain squished beneath Jesse's feet like a wet sponge. He noticed freshly placed flowers on each of the stones and wondered if his were good enough. He had brought a simple bouquet of roses, carnations, and other flowers he couldn't name. Not that Robbie would care, but Jesse still felt like he needed to do more for the one person who had sacrificed everything for him, including his own life.

He rounded the corner of a large stone and froze. A woman with long dark hair and a fashionable hat stood in front of his brother's grave. Jesse took a few steps closer and watched as the woman removed a tissue from her purse and wiped her face. "Rachael?"

She turned to face Jesse with eyes stained red from tears. "Hi, Jesse. I was just finishing. I'll leave you alone."

She started to walk away. Jesse said, "Please wait." She stopped and turned back to Jesse. "How have you been?" he asked.

Rachael shrugged. "Okay. You?"

"Okay." Jesse turned to Robbie's stone and noticed the large arrangement of fresh flowers. "Is that from you?"

Rachael nodded.

Jesse had been picking up and dropping off Emma at the flower shop every other weekend for the past six months, and each time Rachael seemed to just be leaving or going into the back of the store whenever he got there, never saying so much as two words to him. It wasn't until now that he realized why. "Those are beautiful. Robbie would've liked them."

"Thank you. One of the perks of working as a florist, I guess."

"Yeah, I guess."

"How's Madison?"

"She's doing great. Looking forward to the summer break."

"I bet."

He noticed the tears welling in her eyes. "You do know that this," he said, motioning to Robbie's grave, "isn't your fault."

Rachael looked down. "If I hadn't walked through that door at that exact moment, he'd be here now. And his little girl wouldn't have to go through life without her…" She paused as if unable to continue.

"You didn't pull the trigger, Rachael. That was Kevin, not you." Tears ran from her eyes like rain breaking loose from the dark clouds above. "Come here," he said, pulling her into his arms. "It's not your fault."

"I was afraid you hated me. Not that I could blame you for that."

"I don't hate you. No one hates you." He pulled back and looked her in the eye. "Robbie died doing what he did best, protecting the ones he loved."

"Yeah," she nodded. "Must run in the family."

Jesse looked back at the glossy stone. "He was something else." He felt Rachael grab his arm.

"Thank you, Jesse."

"Don't mention it. I guess I'll see you this weekend."

"What do you mean?"

"At the flower shop? When I pick up Emma?"

"I quit."

"What? When?"

"Today was my last day. I told Sarah a few weeks ago that I was quitting, but I wanted to give her some time to replace me. The new girl starts tomorrow, so today was my last day."

"Wow. I'm so…surprised. What are you planning on doing now?"

"I am officially going back to school. The flower business was always Sarah's dream. I was always tagging along, afraid to have dreams of my own or afraid of failing. Either way, the one thing this whole tragedy has taught me is that life is short. And I want to find my own way."

"Well, I'm happy for you. Shocked, but happy for you. Good luck with school."

"Thanks." She flashed a smile. "You should do the same."

"I don't think so. I'm done with school. Besides, I really like what I do."

She shook her head. "That's not what I'm talking about."

Like being on the clueless end of a joke, Jesse didn't understand what she was talking about.

"Life is short. Jesse, how long are you going to keep pushing Sarah away?"

"What are you talking about?"

"Come on, Jesse. You're a smart guy. Don't you think it's strange that Sarah hasn't dated or so much as talked to another man in the past six months?"

"What?"

"That's right. She's still in love with you."

"Sarah and I have a very complicated past. And now there's Emma and Madison."

"I know. And here you both stand. That same past that has brought you two together, the one that has given you love that most people only dream of finding, is the wall that stands between you now."

Jesse ran a hand through his hair. "There's just too much at stake now. And every time we've tried to be together, life has separated us." He looked down at the flowers in his hand. "I don't think I could take that again."

"She's not going anywhere, Jesse. She's waiting for you. She's waiting for you now. Don't throw away this love. Don't waste this life." She looked at Robbie's grave. "It's a gift, Jesse. And we never know how long it will last."

Epilogue

Sarah & Jesse

Beneath the willow, three months later

A cool breeze sent the lazy willow tree's branches dancing above. Sarah drew in a deep breath and let out a sigh. The heavy chains of the city had fallen away somewhere between Chicago and the Welcome to New Haven sign. Time slowed with the soothing sound of the running creek. No e-mails to check. No customers to help. No floral arrangements to plan. Nothing to plan at all. A nice break from the busy chaos of life.

Willow trotted over to the creek and took a drink. Then he set his wet mouth and nose on Sarah's lap. "Are you bored?" She picked up a stick and heaved it, sending Willow on a chase.

Sarah glanced over at her mother who looked as out of place as she'd ever seen her, a fishing pole in one hand. Her mother carefully brought the pole back and then let it rip. The hook caught hold of one of the hanging branches above, causing a few leaves to cascade down, but refusing to release its hold on the branch. Sarah tried not to laugh and ended up coughing instead.

"What's so funny?" her mother demanded. "So my aim's not perfect yet. Give me a chance."

"Practice makes perfect," she said as she drew back her own pole and sent the hook into the middle of the creek.

"No one likes a showoff." Evelyn stood up and removed the hook from the branch, bringing down a few more leaves in the process.

Willow returned with the stick and dropped it next to Sarah. She gave it another toss. "Do you need some help with that, Mom?"

"I'll manage. This isn't my first time fishing, you know. But probably my second," she added.

"Well, you're doing great."

"This was always your father's thing. He tried to get me to go with him, but after I fell into the creek the first time, I kind of lost the drive for it."

Sarah chuckled. "I wish I could have been there."

Evelyn glared at Sarah.

"What? I meant for moral support."

"I know what you meant. And don't get your hopes up about seeing me in the water today either."

Sarah patted the ground next to her. "Why don't you put that down and sit next to me? You won't be able to fall in over here."

Evelyn set down her pole with part of a branch still stuck to the hook. "That'll be the most I'll catch all day."

"That's okay," Sarah said. "I'm just glad you came along. I needed a break from the city. This is Jesse's weekend with Emma, and I would have gone crazy sitting around the house."

"How is that working out with Jesse?"

"Good. He loves Emma so much, and I can tell that she's crazy about him."

"He seems like a good guy."

One of the best, Sarah thought. "I'm just happy that Emma has him. Especially after what happened with Kevin."

"That little girl has been through a lot, but she's tough, like her mother." Evelyn put her arm around Sarah and gave her a squeeze.

"I get that from you."

Willow returned with the stick, but this time, he set it next to Evelyn. "You are a gorgeous dog," she said, rubbing behind his ears. Then she looked at Sarah. "Your strength comes from your father. He was the strongest man I've ever known."

Sarah thought about all the times she and her father had fished this spot. More times than she could count. He could sit for hours and not say a word. She could always tell that he had a lot on his mind. When he did talk though, he had a soft, gentle voice. A relaxing tone that always reminded her of wisdom and patience. "I miss him."

"So do I." Evelyn's smile faded as her gaze shifted toward the creek. "You know what he said to me when you took your first steps?"

Sarah shook her head.

"He must have walked you up and down the hallway a hundred times that day, with your tiny hands wrapped around his fingers. He said that until then, he had never seen someone as beautiful as me."

She looked at Sarah with tears in her eyes. "And he was right. You were so…beautiful."

"Aw. Thank you." Sarah set down her pole and put an arm around her mom. "Now I definitely got that from you."

"I loved your father so much, Sarah. I don't ever want you to doubt that."

"I know you did." She looked her mom in the eye. "And Dad knows, too."

Her mom pulled a tissue from her pocket and wiped her eyes. "What am I going to do with you, Sarah?"

"What do you mean?"

"I worry about you, honey."

"You don't have to worry about me. The business is doing great. Emma's doing great. She's happy. And now she has Jesse."

"But you don't."

Sarah pulled back, looking out toward the creek. She loved Jesse. Probably always would. But things between them had changed. "It's okay, Mom."

"Is it? Every time he comes by and I'm around, I see a different Sarah. You become so…different. I can tell that you love him."

Willow stood up and took off running into the woods behind them.

"Willow! Get back here!" Evelyn shouted.

"It's okay. I always let him run when we come out here. He's probably chasing a squirrel."

Her mom turned back to look at her. "I just don't want to see you ending up like I did."

"What do you mean?"

"Wasting years not being with the one you love. The one you know you should be with."

"Jesse and I have tried to be together before. And it didn't end well."

"Not by any of your doing. Those things were unfortunate, but it doesn't mean you simply give up. That's the mistake I made."

"I haven't given up. Listen, it's complicated."

"All good things are. But it's worth the try."

"I have tried." Sarah felt a lump form in the back of her throat.

"You have?"

She nodded. "I've reached out to him. I've let him know that I'm here for him. But he doesn't reach back."

In a soft tone, her mother asked, "Have you told him that you love him?"

Sarah looked down at the ground beneath her. The same place where she and Jesse used to play as children. Where they had their first kiss. Where they made love for the first time. The place where she now finally realized that she might never be with him again. She shook her head, and tears fell to the ground.

Her mother put an arm around her and looked around. "What is it with this place? It's…it's…"

"Magical," Sarah answered.

She felt the nudge of Willow's cold nose. "Hey, boy. Did you find a squirrel?"

"Excuse me, ma'am, but is this your dog?"

***

Jesse tried to give his best impersonation of a police officer, but he came off sounding more like a government agent instead.

"Jesse?" Sarah shot up. She wiped her eyes, and he could tell she'd been crying. "What are you doing here? Is Emma okay?"

"Mommy!" Emma ran up to Sarah and wrapped her arms around her waist.

"Hey, sweetie! It's so good to see you." She knelt down to give her a hug. "What are you guys doing here?" she asked again.

"It's a surprise, Mommy."

"Well, I'm definitely surprised." She looked over at Madison, who stood next to Jesse, holding his hand. "Hi, Maddie."

Maddie smiled at her. "Hi! Can I pet Willow?"

"Of course you can. He'd like that."

Madison walked over to Willow and ran a tiny hand down his back. Willow's tail flipped back and forth in appreciation.

Sarah looked up at Jesse. "How did you know I was here?"

Jesse glanced over at Sarah's mom, who smiled. "Let's just say I had an informant."

"An informant, huh?" Sarah looked at her mom. "I wonder who that could be."

"You two look like you have plenty to talk about. Girls? Would you like to go fishing with me?"

"Yes, please!" Emma and Maddie shouted, running to Evelyn.

Sarah's mom picked up two poles, and the girls followed with Willow trotting behind them.

"Wow," Jesse said. "This place looks the same." The willow tree stood as tall as ever. Unaffected by time. "Look at that," he said, pointing to the carving.

"I remember when you did that." Sarah traced the letters with her finger. "J&S 4-ever."

"So much has changed."

"Some of it good," Sarah answered, looking over at the girls who were running in circles around her mom.

"Definitely."

She turned back to Jesse. "You never said what brought you here."

Jesse held up an old tackle box. "Fishing."

"Where's your fishing pole?"

Jesse motioned behind him. "I forgot it. I'm still trying to get used to having two little girls to get ready when we go somewhere. I almost left my place without shoes today."

Sarah laughed. "I have an extra." She picked up a green fishing pole and held it out to him. "You can use it if you want to."

"Are you sure?"

She nodded. "It was my dad's. It just didn't feel right not bringing it."

Jesse took the pole and examined it. "This is nice. Thanks. So, do you come here a lot?"

She shook her head. "Only when I need a break from the city."

"I know what you mean. Whenever I feel the pressure getting to me, I think about your father's garden and how peaceful that was. A piece of country in the middle of the city."

Sarah sat down and leaned against the willow tree. Jesse sat next to her. "I loved that garden. I miss it. It reminded me of this place."

Jesse looked up at the tree's drooping branches swaying side to side. "I sure have missed this place. I wish

I could bottle it and take it back to the city." He breathed in the fresh air and turned toward Sarah. Butterflies danced in his stomach at the sight of her. Rays of sunlight shone through the branches, highlighting her blonde hair. He wanted to slide his hand across the soft skin of her cheek and feel her arms wrapped tightly around him.

"What?" she asked. "Is something wrong?"

"Actually, there is."

"What is it?"

"I need some bait."

She held up a small white tub of dirt and worms. "We were using these. Not that we had much luck with them. The only thing we've caught so far is a branch."

"A branch?"

"It's a long story."

"I have something I prefer using over live bait. But it's in my tackle box. Would you mind getting it for me?"

"Not at all." Sarah stood up and walked over to the old tackle box. "What is it I'm looking for in here?"

"You'll know when you see it."

Jesse set the fishing pole down and watched as Sarah opened the box. She reached inside and pulled out a piece of paper. Jesse's heart raced as he stood up and walked over to her.

"What's this?" she asked. "This paper has my name on it."

Jesse shrugged. "Is there anything else in there?"

She smiled and looked back into the box. The only thing left was a wooden box that looked as if it had been carved by hand. She pulled it out. "Is this some kind of joke? Is something going to jump out at me?"

Jesse took the box from her. "No, this is definitely not a joke." He watched as her smile faded, leaving her looking as serious as the ache he felt in his chest. "There's something I have to tell you."

"What is it? Is everything okay?

Jesse took a deep breath and pushed away his fears, his anxieties, his insecurities.

"From the first moment I met you, with those silly yellow rubber rain boots you wore, I knew that I was hopelessly in love with you. The way you smile, the way you laugh, the selfless way you put others' needs ahead of your own, and now the way you care for our daughter are all things that I love about you. But the thing I love most is the way you make me feel every time we are together."

"Jesse?"

"Please, just let me finish. I have to get this out."

Sarah nodded.

Jesse slid open a side compartment on the box and removed an object, closing his hand around it. He got down on one knee, looked at Sarah, and opened his hand to reveal a diamond ring. Her mother's ring. The ring they found the night they dug up the time capsule, the same night Emma was conceived.

She placed a hand over her mouth and tears welled in her eyes. "How did you get that?"

"My informant has been extremely helpful," he replied. "When I placed this ring on your finger all those years ago, I wanted nothing more than for you to be my wife. I know that our story together has been full of obstacles and tragedy, but it's been full of love, too. Love so great that I don't ever want to live without it again. And

I'm willing to fight for that love. I'm willing to fight for you, Sarah." With his heart pounding in his chest, Jesse brought up the ring. "Sarah, if you marry me, I can't promise you a life without storms, but I can promise you that I will love with you everything that's inside of me and that no matter what storms come our way, I'll never stop loving you. I'll never let you go."

Sarah looked at the ring, and then at Jesse. She smiled through her tears. "Jesse Malone, what took you so long? Of course I'll marry you."

The weight of the world fell from Jesse's shoulders as his heart swelled with happiness. He slid the ring on her finger and then picked her up, spinning her beneath the willow tree.

"I love you, Sarah."

Her lips touched his and the electricity shot through his body like a wave of heat. "And I love you, Jesse. I can't believe this is happening. I didn't think you had any feelings left for me anymore."

"I've always loved you, Sarah. I tried letting you go. I tried burying those feelings and moving on with my life." He shrugged. "But every time I see you, they come back so forcefully that I…" He paused and pushed a few strands of her hair to the side. "I'm done fighting them, Sarah. I love you so much, and I don't want to waste another second of my life without you."

"Jesse Malone, I don't know what to say except that you have made me the happiest woman in the world." They sat beneath the willow tree, holding each other as they watched Evelyn and the girls fish. The girls giggled when Evelyn got her hook stuck in a branch again. Madison leaned over and whispered something into Emma's ear, causing her to laugh.

Jesse savored the moment. A lifetime had passed since he and Robbie had shared moments like these. Living carelessly through the innocent eyes of children, oblivious to the storms of life. Sadness filled him. His mom and his brother had both been taken from him, and he had only memories of them now. All the times he'd heard the boisterous laughter of his older brother. The security he had felt in Robbie's strength. He missed his older brother and knew then that the hole he had left in Jesse's heart would never be filled. He had lost his best friend—his brother— the one person who had been with him since the beginning. The same person who would be telling him now to enjoy every minute of this life. *I hear ya, big brother*, he thought.

He turned to Sarah, taking in the smell of her hair and those lips, the same lips he had shared his first kiss with. He'd had no idea then what kind of journey life had in store for them. The ups and the downs and the separations. At the age of twelve, he had fallen in love with Sarah, and in many ways, he had never stopped.

Their eyes locked and for a moment, he could see the hunger in Sarah's eyes. The same hunger that burned inside of him. She touched a place inside of him where no one had ever been before. He gazed at her. Her crystal blue eyes reflected the flowing creek next to them. A dream, he thought. No, he'd never had a dream quite this wonderful.

"What are you thinking about?" Sarah asked.

Jesse was thinking about his Aunt Sherry and a favorite quote of hers. He could almost hear that lyrical tone she used: *Life doesn't always give you what you want.*

But it always gives you what you need... He turned to Sarah and replied, "How wonderful you are and how unbelievably happy I am."

"Me, too." She nuzzled into his shoulder. "I've never been happier."

Whoever had said it was right, he thought as he watched the girls fishing. Life didn't always give you what you wanted. Sometimes, just sometimes...it gave you more.

~

Want to read more by Jeremy Asher? Like him on Facebook or check out his website at www.jeremyasherauthor.com for news on previously published and upcoming novels.

Other works by Jeremy Asher
Across the Creek
Insignificant Moments
Losing Faith

Continue reading for a sneak peek at *Losing Faith*, Asher's latest novel.

Chapter 1

Seth Storm

December 22nd

Rain fell onto Seth's car, creating tiny explosions of water on his windshield. He turned a dial, and his windshield wipers flipped back and forth. A large bolt of lightning raced across the sky, sending a chill down his back. He checked the clock on the dash and tightened his grip on the steering wheel as he pressed down on the accelerator, pushing his Mustang through the storm. The orange needle of his speedometer climbed in response. In about forty minutes, he'd be on a plane heading back to Fort Wayne, Indiana. The one place he had spent his entire life trying to leave was now the place he had to get back to. Although Nashville had been the home where Seth Storm had made his lifelong dreams come true, those same dreams had taken away the one thing he simply couldn't live without.

Lightning lit up the sky once again, revealing flashes of the barren country road. Seth turned to look at the weathered guitar case sitting in the passenger seat. Scratches and splintered wood told the story of the years of hardship and strife that had led to the fame he once coveted and now resented. Everything about that old guitar case represented everything he hated about himself, except for one tiny part, a picture of his daughter, Faith, taped to the side next to the handle. He remembered the day that picture had been taken. Faith had just finished singing in the school

Christmas program. It had been her first concert. She had a solo, and he remembered how quiet the crowd had become the moment her angelic voice rang out over the auditorium. She had captivated everyone, the same way she had captivated him since her birth.

Through the good, the bad, the success, and the failure, Faith had been there for all of it, loving him no matter what. Now it was time for him to be there for her. And nothing could stop him from getting back to her. He had made a promise to her, and he wasn't about to let her down. Not this time.

Thunder roared like a lion's battle cry. Seth gripped the wheel and looked up into the darkness. "I'm coming, Faith."

After a series of rapid flashes, the rain intensified, as if the lightning had somehow ripped a hole in the hidden clouds above, releasing buckets of rain. He turned up his wipers, but they did little to clear his view. He looked back at the clock on the dash. Time was running out. He had to make his flight.

Another flash lit up the sky, and Seth saw that he wasn't alone on the road anymore. He saw a set of taillights in a ditch. He drove past, not taking his foot off the gas. He didn't have time for this now. Besides, someone else would drive down this same road and be able to help.

He stared into his rearview mirror, expecting to see another car traveling down the same road, but it was just as dark as the road ahead. His hands gripped the wheel again, and then he slammed on the brakes, sliding to a stop. The Mustang purred as he debated whether he should get involved or not. This isn't your problem, he told himself.

Think about Faith. You can't be late. And you *will* be late if you don't keep driving.

Seth closed his eyes and tightened his jaw. He smacked his hand on the wheel, unable to contain his frustration. Then he slid the car into reverse and backed up to the red car sitting in the shallow ditch.

The car's taillights and headlights were both on, and smoke billowed from the tailpipe. From where he sat, it didn't appear that anyone was inside. Seth looked around and saw nothing but darkness in every direction. The car was obviously still running. Why would its owner leave it?

He looked to the road ahead, which held his last chance to make his flight and finally get his life back on track. Then he took another look at the little red car in the ditch. He clutched the wheel until his knuckles turned white. "Just go," he murmured. This is someone else's problem. Besides, he thought, staring at the picture of Faith, his little girl is depending on him. He couldn't let her down again. He had promised her, and broken promises had cost him enough in life. His foot settled on the gas pedal, but he didn't have it in him to put the car in drive. He stared at the disabled vehicle. Rain bounced from its roof, and he wished more than anything that it would wash the little red car away. The pit in his stomach turned into a large boulder as he realized what he had to do.

He backed up and parked on the shoulder of the road. He pulled out his cell phone and saw that he only had one bar. He popped open the glove box to the Mustang and found only the manual. Remembering to bring a cell phone charger was something his wife, Lexi, had always done. She had always been the responsible one. He stared at the phone's screen. This is it, he thought. Better make it count. He looked over at the little red car, took a deep breath, and dialed.

"This is 9-1-1. Please state your emergency." The stoic male voice on the other end seemed removed from the stress Seth was feeling.

"There's been a car accident. I need you to send help."

"What is your location, sir?"

"My location?" He looked around, trying to get his bearings. "I'm on Leafland Road." He heard the clacking of keys in the background.

"Can you be more specific?"

"I'm in the country. There's nothing but fields and trees. I can't be any more specific than that."

"Are you hurt, sir?"

"No," Seth shook his head. "I wasn't in the accident. I was on my way to the airport when I noticed a car in the ditch."

"Is anyone hurt?"

Seth turned to the red car. "I can't tell. It's pretty dark here and raining hard. I can't tell if anyone is inside the car or not."

More clacking of the keys. "Was there another vehicle involved?"

"I don't think so. At least, there aren't any other vehicles around. Are you guys sending someone out here or what?"

"I've dispatched someone to your location. They should be there in about twenty minutes."

"Twenty minutes!"

"Yes, sir. There are a lot of accidents tonight due to the storm."

His pulse raced as he looked at the time on the dash. He didn't have twenty minutes. He didn't have five for that matter.

"Sir?"

Seth released the breath he had been holding. "Yes?"

"I need to get some more information from you."

Seth heard a faint beep. He checked his screen. The low battery indicator flashed.

"Okay, but my battery is about to go dead."

"Do you have a charger on you?"

"No," he answered. "And I'm in the middle of nowhere, so I don't have a way to charge it either."

"What's your name?"

"Seth Storm."

The clacking ceased for a moment before starting back up again. He wondered for a moment if the dispatcher believed him, or if he thought that Seth didn't want to tell him his *real* name.

"Where exactly is your vehicle located now?"

"I'm parked on the side of the road, about five to ten feet from the car in the ditch." His phone beeped again.

"And you said that you can't see anyone in it?"

"That's right." He looked at the car and leaned across his guitar, trying to get a better look. "It's really dark out here, and the rain is coming down hard." Another beep reminded Seth that the rain was the least of his problems now.

"Is there anyone else with you? Has anyone else stopped to help?"

He wanted to ask him why he would ask that question, but time was running out. All he wanted to do was get back on the road and away from this nightmare. He looked down the desolate road. Darkness had swallowed anything resembling civilization. "No. It's just me." *Beep.*

"And you're sure you can't see anyone else in the other vehicle? No movement at all?"

"I already told you, it's dark and it's raining. I can't see much of anything right now. You're wasting time."

"It's important that you remain calm, Seth. I am just trying to gather as much information as I can to prepare the emergen…"

"Hello?" Seth looked at his screen, only to find it void of life. He tossed his phone over to the seat next to him and stared at the red car through the passenger-side window. Smoke continued to rise from its tailpipe, turning red as it passed in front of the taillights. If the driver had abandoned the vehicle, then why hadn't he turned off his car? A feeling of dread settled in his stomach, making him queasy. "Because the driver never left." He answered his own question.

He looked up and down the road for signs of help or, at the very least, a passing car. But it was as if everyone knew not to travel down this road, at this time of night, in this kind of storm. Everyone except the driver of the red car and Seth. He knew he should get out of his car and check it out, but he wasn't trained for this type of situation. He was a musician for crying out loud, not a rescue worker. Besides, if he left now, he'd probably make his flight. If someone ever questioned him, he'd just tell the truth, that he'd done everything he could. After all, he was the one who had called for help. He glanced at the useless phone sitting on the passenger seat next to his guitar case and then over at the red car. His heart stopped and fell into his stomach. He could see the silhouette of a head in the driver's seat.

Seth opened his car door and took his first steps into the cold rain. It ran down his head, instantly soaking his hair, pushing it into his forehead and eyes. Smoky breaths disappeared into the dark as he made his way over to the other car. A large flash of lightning startled him, but he kept walking forward. His nerves tingled with electricity as if charged by the storm itself. He or she is probably okay, he thought. Probably just in shock from the accident. But the closer he got, the heavier his heart felt. The front end of the car had crumpled like an accordion against a large rock on the far side of the ditch.

A small figure sat hunched over the steering wheel. Seth froze in the pouring rain, waiting to see if the driver would move. He knew he had to do something, so he placed his cold, numb hand on the door handle and gave it a tug. It opened with the first pull. The light inside the red car came on, revealing a woman. Her head rested on its side on the steering wheel with a half-inflated air bag in front of her. What he could see of her face was free from wrinkles and age. That and her trendy clothes had him guessing early twenties at the oldest.

"Are you okay?" he asked.

She didn't respond, and he wondered if she was sleeping. He hoped she was just sleeping. He scanned the rest of her—what he could see without moving her—for injury. Relief washed over him. No blood. No bones sticking out of her. Small pieces of glass spilled out onto the dashboard and passenger seat. He took a step closer but drew back instantly and tried to keep himself from throwing up. A piece of wood from a structure he couldn't make out had broken apart and was now sticking out from the woman's right side.

Seth pressed his right hand into his stomach and ran back to his car. He took a few deep breaths, but the image of the wood sticking out of her side kept popping into his mind. His stomach tightened and then released as everything inside it came up, burning his throat.

After a few painful moments, he stood up and leaned against his car. The cold rain did little to cool his nerves. He stared at the red car while he took a few more deep breaths and gathered himself. Then he opened his door and picked up the phone.

He tried to turn on the power, hoping for the slightest bit of power to make another phone call, but the screen lit up for just a second or two before powering down again. He tossed the phone back into the car.

Seth rubbed his hands together to get warm, but it did little against the persistent downpour of cold rain. The darkness of the night combined with the fury of the storm had him craving a drink. A road he couldn't afford to go down again. He instinctively looked in the back seat, as if expecting to find a partial bottle that had been rolling around on the floor, but they had all been removed the day he checked himself into rehab. A day he'd never forget. The first day of the longest journey of his life. And the day he had lost everything. He rubbed a tattoo of flames on the back of his left hand.

The sky flashed, and rumbling thunder followed. Seth turned back to the red car. I shouldn't be here right now, he thought. Instead he should be on a plane, on his way back to Faith. His little girl. Then he thought about the young woman in the car. Injured. Possibly dying. She was someone's little girl, too, he thought. And now she's trapped in that car. In this storm. Alone.

He headed back to the red car. He peeked inside the window to see if anything had changed, trying to avoid seeing the wood protruding from her side. But she was still in the same position. He opened the door slowly. The dome light came back on. He knelt down closer, looking for any signs of life. He listened for breathing, but the rain and wind created too much noise. He pressed two fingers gently against her neck, feeling for a pulse. Nothing. He checked again, pressing harder, and this time he felt something. A faint pulse beat beneath his fingertips.

Seth pushed a few strands of dark hair from the woman's face. Her porcelain skin felt cold to the touch. He stood up and removed his jacket, placing it gently around her shoulders, careful not to disturb her too much. He looked down the road, hoping to see flashing lights.

"Come on, guys," he murmured. "Get here."

"Who are you?"

Seth turned back and found the young woman's large blue eyes open and staring at him. "I'm Seth," he said. "What's your name?"

"Melanie," she said. She tried to sit up and winced from the pain. "Why can't I sit up?"

Seth took a look at the wood on her other side and then crouched down in front of her, placing his hand on her back. "You've been in an accident, Melanie. Do you remember any of that?"

She nodded. "I thought I saw a dog or something run out in front of me, so I swerved and lost control. I tried to straighten the car, but I ended up in this ditch."

Tears welled in her eyes and slid down the side of her face.

Seth rubbed her back. "It's okay now. I've called 9-1-1, and help is on the way."

"Thank you." Her shaky voice rose just above a whisper. "Will you stay with me?"

Will you stay with me? The same question Faith had asked him just before she went on stage to perform at her first concert. A question that had broken his heart then, just as it did now.

He nodded and grabbed her hand. "Of course I will, Melanie. I'm not going anywhere. I promise."

A faint smile formed on her face, and she closed her eyes. "Melanie. Melanie!" Seth didn't know much about first aid, but he knew if she had a concussion, it'd be better if she stayed awake. He squeezed her hand, and her eyes opened again. "You should stay awake."

"I'm so tired," she whispered.

"I know. But help is on the way. It'll be here before you know it."

She nodded and looked up at his face. "You're wet."

He no longer felt the rain that continued to drench him. He ran a hand through his soaked hair. "Yeah, not much I can do about that now."

"You look familiar." She studied his face.

"I get that a lot," he said, hoping she wouldn't figure out who he was, or worse yet, who he used to be.

"Are you a singer?"

He let out a sigh. "I used to be."

Melanie's eyes trailed down and settled on his necklace. "That's beautiful," she said.

"You like it?" He took it off and held up the gold guitar pick pendant. He ran his thumb over the words, remembering the day his wife had given it to him. The same day he had decided to give up on his lifelong dreams of making it in the music industry.

"What does it say?" she asked.

Seth read the inscription aloud. "To have a dream is good. To chase one is better."

Melanie smiled. "I like that."

Seth reached down and opened Melanie's hand, placing the necklace inside.

"What are you doing? I can't accept this."

"I made you a promise, and I kept it. I'm still here." He closed her fingers around the necklace. "Now I need you to make me a promise. I need you to stay here with me. I need you to get better, and then someday you can return it to me. Can you do that?"

Her hand squeezed the necklace, tears welling in her eyes. "I will. I promise."

Seth placed his hand gingerly on her back. A flash of light reflecting off the metal of her car caught his eye.

He stood and turned around. An ambulance and a couple of police cars were heading their way. Relief filled his tense muscles, and his jaw tightened as he bit back tears.

"Can you see that, Melanie? Soon you'll be out of here."

But she didn't respond, and her eyes were closed. "Melanie, did you hear me? You're getting out of here." He fell to his knees and placed his hand on her back. "Melanie!"

Her eyes opened, but something was missing. The light within her blue eyes was all but gone now. The large pit returned to Seth's stomach, and he wanted to throw up again. He had to do something. She had to make it. He couldn't let her down. Not her, too. Not now. "Melanie! Stay with me. You promised."

Her eyes shut and then opened again. He wanted to scream. He wanted to run. He wanted to do something, anything to get her back. "Hold on!" he shouted. Then the golden guitar pick fell from her hand and swung from the chain still wrapped around her fingers. Tears ran down his cheeks and washed away with the rain. "Melanie! Hold on!"

~

Want to read more? *Losing Faith* is now available through Amazon.

F   Asher, Jeremy.
ASH   Beneath the willow

Made in the USA
Lexington, KY
28 June 2014